The
Beloved
Dearly

The Beloved Dearly

Doug Cooney

Simon & Schuster Books for Young Readers

New York   London   Toronto   Sydney   Singapore

SIMON & SCHUSTER BOOKS FOR YOUNG READERS
An imprint of Simon & Schuster Children's Publishing Division
1230 Avenue of the Americas, New York, New York 10020
Text copyright © 2002 by Doug Cooney
Illustrations copyright © 2002 by Tony DiTerlizzi
All rights reserved, including the right of reproduction in whole or in part in any form.
SIMON & SCHUSTER BOOKS FOR YOUNG READERS is a trademark of Simon & Schuster.

Book design by Anahid Hamparian
The text for this book is set in 14-point Revival.
Printed in the United States of America

4 6 8 10 9 7 5 3

Library of Congress Cataloging-in-Publication Data
Cooney, Doug.
The beloved dearly / by Doug Cooney.
p. cm.
Summary: Although his father has forbidden it, Ernie, a twelve-year-old business tycoon,
makes a tidy profit in the pet funeral business, but when he refuses to give his star employee
a raise and the business starts to fall apart, it takes the death of his own dog
to bring everyone back together.
ISBN 0-689-83127-7
[1. Business enterprises—Fiction. 2. Funeral rites and ceremonies—Fiction. 3. Pets—Fiction.
4. Fathers and sons—Fiction.] I. Title.
PZ7.C7837 Be 2002
[Fic]—dc21
2001020308

World Premiere Production by TADA! in New York City
Artistic Director: Janine Nina Trevens

For CCML

The author gratefully acknowledges Beverly Emmons, Elizabeth Swados, Ted Cooney, Carling Boyles, and the many creative artists of all ages who have contributed their energy and spirit to this story.

Contents

Chapter One

The Action

𝓔rnie looked like a total teacher's pet, standing at the blackboard in a clean shirt with his hair combed flat. He was reciting a book report on Benjamin Franklin as though he were the best student in school. "In the words of Benjamin Franklin," Ernie read from his notebook, "'Time is money.'"

Ms. Pringle was certainly impressed. She was nodding, smiling, and totally buying the whole Benjamin Franklin thing—but if she'd seen Ernie during lunch break, she'd have seen a different Ernie altogether.

Ernie had caused a royal ruckus. Cafeteria Lady was scooping heaps of mystery meat onto the kids' trays when suddenly Ernie climbed right on top of a cafeteria table. He planted his feet firmly between a couple kids' cafeteria trays. "Cheeseburgers!" he hollered like a ballpark vendor. "Only one dollar! Get your red-hot cheeseburgers!"

Ernie opened a large fast-food bag he'd had clamped under one arm and started tossing burgers right and left. The kids went wild. Ernie scrambled to collect all the dollar bills that were being thrust at him.

The event should have been a huge money-maker. Ernie stood to make a lot of quick cash. But then catastrophe struck.

One burger splattered against the wall. Another burger struck the overhead fan and burst into pieces. Yet another burger caught Cafeteria Lady right in the kisser. And basically what happened after that was Ernie landed in the principal's office.

Mr. Bridwell, the principal, had seen plenty of Ernie. He had heard all the stories. Ernie was the kind of kid who would drain the lunch money out of every student in the school. Ernie would sell the lawn chair from under his grandmother. The boy was just a natural-born salesman.

"Ernie," Mr. Bridwell said, "you really broke the rules this time."

"I wasn't breaking the rules, Mr. Bridwell," Ernie protested. "I was obeying the law of supply and demand!"

The principal sighed. "I think maybe we should redirect your 'entrepreneurial enthusiasm' toward something more 'appropriate'—like the school fund-raising drive." Mr. Bridwell had a habit of indicating every quotation mark in his speech by wagging his fingers in the air.

Ernie threw his hands up in despair. "Bridwell!" he barked. "You're killing me with the nickel-and-dime stuff! Cookie dough, chocolate, calendars! Don't even mention magazine subscriptions!" He perched on the edge of the principal's desk. "I believe in charity, Bridwell. But I'm a businessman. And if you wanna work the kid angle, you gotta cut us in on the *action*."

"What 'action'?" Mr. Bridwell asked, with another wag of his fingers.

"The bank, the beans, the jimmy, the jive. The moola, the greenbacks, the dead presidents!" Ernie cried. He was talking about money.

Mr. Bridwell was positively flummoxed.

After the "dead presidents" remark, it was all over for Ernie, except for a detention, a blue slip, and a telephone call to Ernie's father.

Ernie's dad, Red, worked at the local sheet metal plant. His shift usually went till five-thirty or six in the evening—but when Red got a phone call from the school, he had to leave work early to bail his kid out of detention. So when Red showed up at the principal's office in his factory uniform and a windbreaker, he was not in a good mood.

Red and Mr. Bridwell had a long talk behind a closed door. Ernie sneaked up to the door and cupped his ear against it with his hands. He was trying to listen, but he couldn't really make out the words.

"Time and time again," he heard Mr. Bridwell say.

His dad said "Cheeseburgers?" two or three times. "Cheeseburgers? Cheeseburgers?" Every time he said it, the idea sounded more and more absurd.

When Ernie heard the doorknob jiggle, he jumped back to his seat. Red walked out of the principal's office and flagged Ernie to follow him.

"That didn't take too long," Ernie said cheerfully. Red just glowered at him.

Red pushed through the office doors and walked down the hall. He didn't even hold the door for Ernie. It bounced back and almost caught him in the nose. Ernie hustled down the hall to match his father's pace, but it wasn't easy to do.

Usually the lecture didn't start until Red got Ernie into the car. This time, however, the lecture started in the hallway.

"Ernie, these get-rich schemes have got to stop! You can't take advantage of people!" Red said.

Ernie tried to protest, but Red didn't leave room for interruption.

"It's not like we haven't been through this time and time before! Used homework, booger insurance, skateboard rentals! They're scams, Ernie! You had to give the money back!"

All Ernie could think of to say was, "But Dad!" And that wasn't saying much.

Red slammed through the crash doors at the end of the hall and stepped into the parking lot. Ernie muttered, "Oh, man," under his breath and pushed through the doors behind him.

Chapter Two

Mister Doggie

$\mathscr{R}$**ed stopped at** the grocery store on the way home.

Ernie and Red had a particular method of grocery shopping. Red would open the door in the freezer section and toss frozen dinners over his shoulder at Ernie. Ernie would catch the boxes and flip them into the grocery cart behind him. That was the program.

Ernie missed the days when he got to ride inside the grocery cart, back when his mom did the shopping. But those days were gone. It was just Ernie and his dad now. And Red didn't let him forget it.

"*I'm* the one who has to work," Red said as he chucked a frozen spaghetti dinner in Ernie's direction. "*I* earn the money. Not *you*. I'm the grown-up. You're the kid."

"But Dad!"

"And if I hear any more cockamamie business schemes, you're *grounded*," Red declared.

Ernie couldn't believe his ears. Grounded? That was the worst punishment in the book.

Usually, if Ernie was in trouble, his dad would say no Game Boy, no allowance, no TV, or no Internet. If Ernie was really in hot water, Red would pile on extra chores, like garbage duty for a week.

Ernie spent so much time racing from Point A to Point B in his life that he couldn't even imagine being grounded. Ernie sputtered but no words came out.

"Grounded and with *no* allowance," Red said to add insult to injury as he slammed the door on the standing freezers.

"But Dad!" Ernie finally protested.

Red put his fingers in his ears and sang, "La, la, la, la, la," in a flat, whiny falsetto like a child. He walked down the aisle, singing loud enough for the whole store to hear.

Ernie snatched the grocery cart with a jerk. "I should never have taught you that thing with the ears," he groused.

While Red paid the cashier, Ernie slipped a small notebook out of his pocket. It was his personal journal and he didn't want Red to see it. The cover read, JOBS FOR ERNIE. He flipped to the last entry on the last page, where he had written the ill-fated word: *cheeseburgers*.

That was a lousy idea, Ernie thought. The

7

whole cheeseburger idea had almost gotten him grounded. With the stub of a pencil, Ernie scratched out the word.

"Come on, Ernie!" Red called.

When Ernie looked up, he saw Red standing halfway through the automatic doors to the parking lot. The doors were bouncing back and forth against the grocery cart full of frozen food.

"Ernie, come on!"

Ernie slipped the notebook back into his hip pocket and ran for the door.

When they got back home, Red and Ernie stood in the same fire brigade formation to unload the groceries. Ernie would reach into the brown paper bags and toss the frozen dinners at Red—who caught the boxes and flipped them into the open freezer.

They were almost finished when a small dog came trotting into the kitchen. He sniffed at the grocery bags and gazed up at Ernie and Red.

"Mister Doggie wants to help," Red said.

Ernie scowled. "You know I can't stand that dog," he muttered.

When the last box was stowed away and the last paper bag was tossed into the recycling bin, Red jerked his head toward Mister Doggie. "Your turn to feed him," he told Ernie.

Fast on his heels, but not fast enough, Ernie said, "Your turn to—dang it!"

This was another game. Whoever named the

household chore first, the other person had to do it. Most of the time, Red won. "I said it first." He smirked. "You lose."

Ernie reached for a fresh sack of dog food. Red nudged the freezer door shut with a hard shove of his shoulder. In the process, a freezer magnet fell off the door. It landed with a loud clatter in Mister Doggie's dish. Ernie and Red both lunged to rescue it.

The magnet was a small plastic picture frame that held a photograph of Red, Ernie, Mister Doggie, and Claire—that was Ernie's mom—back in happier days.

Ernie handed the photo to Red but said nothing. Ernie's mom was a sore subject, and he didn't want his dad to talk about it just now. Red took the plastic frame in his hands and replaced the magnet on the freezer without saying a word.

"Be nice to Mister Doggie," Red said. "He goes to the vet tomorrow."

"Again?" Ernie asked. It seemed like Mister Doggie was always going to the hospital.

Red reached down to scruff Mister Doggie's head. "Old and getting older. Stupid dog," he said. "I could have him, you know, put to sleep. . . ."

His voice trailed off as though he didn't want to finish that thought. He paused, then said, "I just can't deal with another funeral right now. Not that we could *afford* another funeral. I'm still paying off the last one."

Pay for a funeral? Ernie stopped pouring dog

food into Mister Doggie's bowl. Was he hearing things? "You had to *pay* for mom's funeral?" he asked.

"You thought they were free?" Red asked over his shoulder.

Ernie backpedaled because he hated sounding like he didn't know something he was supposed to know. "No, I thought they were . . . ," he blurted out defensively, then his voice trailed off.

"Nobody works for free, Ernie," Red said. "Funeral guys make a bundle, believe you me." He grabbed a dog biscuit from the fresh bag and wagged it at Mister Doggie. "Don't they, Mister Doggie? Don't they?" he continued. "A bundle."

Mister Doggie nodded energetically and Red laughed.

"Stupid dog," Ernie muttered.

While Ernie wasn't looking, Red slipped another biscuit into his pocket for later. Mister Doggie had noticed the extra biscuit and he let out a whimper. On the sly, Red winked at Mister Doggie and mouthed the words "For later."

"Your turn to walk him," Red called out as he left the kitchen and headed down the hall.

Fast on his heels, Ernie blurted out, "Your turn to . . ."

But again, not fast enough. "Oh, man," Ernie muttered, reaching for the dog leash and a biscuit.

Mister Doggie nodded.

Chapter Three

A Secret Place

Dusk was settling over the neighborhood when Ernie slipped out the back door with Mister Doggie on the leash.

Ernie lived in a tightly packed block of row houses on Fuller Street. The neighborhood was mostly blue collar—which meant the moms and dads tended to work in factories. The row houses were stodgy old brownstones that had been built forty, fifty, some even sixty, years ago.

A service alley ran behind the houses on Ernie's block, and Mister Doggie knew the routine. Ernie took the back steps two at a time, forcing Mister Doggie to move double time on his little dog legs. When they reached the fence that led to the alley, Mister Doggie automatically turned to the right.

Walking down the alley, Ernie noticed the gingerbread details on the rooftops of the adjoining brownstones. Ernie's mom had always referred to these houses as "the Dowagers." It was another word for "old ladies." When Ernie asked why, Ernie's mom said, "'Cause they're old and crotchety." Ernie still didn't really get the joke. But nowadays, whenever Ernie saw the Dowagers, he was always reminded of his mom.

And in fact, as he was looking up at the rooftops, he heard a young mother's voice yell, "Suppertime! Come to supper!" Ernie thought he was hearing things. But then he heard the mother call the name, "Dusty! Dust-eee!"

Ernie wrapped Mister Doggie's leash over his shoulder and rose on tiptoe to peek over the back fence of a house three doors down. A scruffy nine-year-old boy had just banged out of a toolshed and was headed obediently up the stairs to the kitchen door.

That must be Dusty, Ernie thought. Dusty was a strange kid. He was holding an elaborate hodge-podge of wire hangers that clanged and clattered. It looked to be a wind chime, but Ernie couldn't honestly say what it was. But whatever it was, it was too big for Dusty. He tripped on the hangers and stumbled on the stairs.

Ernie would have laughed when Dusty tripped, but at that same moment, Mister Doggie yanked him away from the fence.

"Easy, Doggie," Ernie protested. But Mister

Doggie was determined to investigate a rusty old gate in a weather-beaten fence that surrounded a lot across the alley. Mister Doggie tugged on the leash and whimpered, sniffing closer and closer toward the gate.

"All right already. Have it your way," Ernie said, letting the dog pull him across the alley.

Ernie stared at the rusty old gate. He'd grown up on this block, but he couldn't honestly recall having noticed this gate ever before. The metal had corroded and the gate was half falling off its post. It was in bad shape. And the lot was so overgrown that Ernie couldn't make out what was on the other side. No light and no sound.

Ernie hooked Mister Doggie to the fence post and, forcing the gate wider, squeezed his way inside. As he nudged against the gate, a faded sign fell off and fluttered to the pavement. Ernie hadn't seen the sign—but it read, NO TRESPASSING.

Ernie crawled through the gnarled bushes inside. When his shirt snagged on a thornbush, he had to wrestle to pull himself free. He tugged and tugged and when he finally tugged hard enough, his shirt ripped away from the branch. Ernie tumbled backward into a small open clearing and landed on the ground.

Ernie sprawled flat on a dry patch of scrappy grass in an empty lot. With the rising moon, the vacant clearing glowed with an eerie, tranquil light.

Even in the dusk, Ernie's face seemed to light

up. It was a moment of discovery. He had found a secret place.

Mister Doggie wandered into the yard as far as his leash would allow. He was growling and snarling as little dogs do. And he pawed and scratched at the sparse patch of dry grass.

"No, Mister Doggie, don't," Ernie said, reaching for the leash. "You're gonna dig up the whole . . ."

Ding! Ernie had an idea.

He paced the property with long strides and stamped at the turf with his sneaker.

Sure, he was thinking. *There's plenty of land. Access from the alley. It's quiet. It's safe.*

With a decisive air, Ernie flipped open his jobs notebook, turned to a blank page, and wrote down the word *funerals*.

Chapter Four

Get to Work

The first thing that Ernie wrote down in his game plan was the word *employees*.

He scrawled it in his notebook under the heading *Things to Do* and he marked it with a star. If Ernie was going to make this project happen, he needed help. The lot was a mess. He couldn't do it all by himself. He needed employees for the dirty work. Ernie thought and thought—and really only one kid came to mind.

Dusty. The strange kid from three doors down.

After his mom died, Ernie had transferred from the Catholic school across town—which was his mom's alma mater—back to the public school in his own neighborhood. "Gotta cut back somewhere," his dad said, meaning the tuition. Ernie didn't mind, except he didn't actually know the kids in his own neighborhood, so all the kids at his new school were basically strangers.

The next afternoon, Ernie tracked down Dusty. He found him leaning over a patch of wet cement in the sidewalk. Ernie ducked behind a tree to see what Dusty was up to.

As Ernie watched, Dusty reached into a large cardboard box beside him and raised an old china plate into the air.

Ernie could never have predicted what happened next.

Dusty smashed the plate against the curb so hard that it shattered into pieces. Then he calmly sifted through the shards until he had selected one particular chip.

Dusty studied the piece closely, rolling it back and forth between his fingers. After some careful thought, he tossed it aside.

When Dusty finally found a shard that was satisfactory, he leaned over the wet cement and carefully pressed the chip into position. For several minutes, he worked in this slow and careful manner.

"This could take forever," Ernie said to himself.

When Dusty was finally done, he sat back to admire his creation. Of course, Ernie had edged closer behind a hedge so that he could see what Dusty was doing. Poking his head through the branches, Ernie saw an elaborate mosaic in the wet cement depicting an intergalactic space battle in wild cartoon colors.

Ernie was impressed. Very impressed.

Unfortunately, a moment later, a boot smashed down right into the middle of the wet cement; a boot belonging to Dion, the neighborhood bully. Dion was a nightmare and a constant threat. Everyone kept wishing he would either grow up or move away. Until that happened, there wasn't much that anyone could do about Dion.

As Dion trampled the wet cement, Dusty flailed helplessly to protect his mosaic.

"Quit! Stop it!"

"Biff! Poweee! Socko! Ooooff!" Dion barked as he stomped.

Ernie ducked inside the hedge. It felt a little cowardly, but Ernie was one to pick his battles wisely.

"Stop! You ruined it!" Dusty cried, pretty much stating the obvious. It was kind of pathetic.

"What are you gonna do, Freakazoid?" Dion snarled.

When the deed was done, Dion charged down the sidewalk. And indeed, the mosaic was demolished. Dusty sat back on his heels, splattered with cement, too wounded to speak, too hurt to cry.

At that moment, a shadow arched over the ruined mosaic. Dusty winced into the sunlight to see who it was.

No surprise here. It was Ernie.

Ernie squatted beside the wet cement and said, "Sweet while it lasted, huh, kid?" He ran his hand over the remnants and continued, "Clever, inventive.

17

Got a sense of humor. And the old plates keep your costs down."

Ernie brushed his hands off and held one out for a handshake. "Good work, kid," he said. "I been looking for a kid like you. Name's Ernie."

"Dusty," said Dusty, wiping off his palm and shaking Ernie's hand.

"Oh, I know your name, all right," said Ernie.

Dusty was bewildered. Nobody in the neighborhood had ever talked to him this way before. They usually just acted as though he was weird.

"I need *boxes*," Ernie announced with a sense of purpose. "Well, not just boxes. More like boxes for a funeral, say."

"For a funeral?" Dusty asked, completely confused. "You mean, you need a coffin?"

"I prefer the word . . . *sarcophagus*," Ernie said with relish. "It's Egyptian. But never mind about that. Got a minute? I got a proposition for you."

And that was how Ernie and Dusty came to be friends.

It was Dusty who tipped Ernie off to Tony. "Look for the kid with the shovel," is what he said. "You can't miss him."

On Dusty's recommendation, Ernie found himself leaning against a lemonade stand late in the afternoon.

Looking across the street, Ernie saw a scrappy little boy, about seven or eight, and sure enough he was flinging a great big shovel, almost twice his size. *That must be Tony,* he thought.

Tony patted down a freshly filled hole and wiped his brow. With the job done, Tony squinted across the street at the lemonade stand and headed in that direction. He dragged the shovel on the pavement behind him and it made an awful sound.

Ernie arranged himself at the counter so that he looked all nonchalant.

Tony arrived and gestured at the Sweaty Lemonade Girl behind the counter. "Hit me with the usual," he said.

Sweaty Lemonade Girl snapped back, "Move along, Stinky. You scare away the customers." She pinched her fingers over her nose and stuck out her tongue.

Tony balked. "Hey," he cried, all indignant and offended, and why shouldn't he be?

Ernie cleared his throat and rolled his eyes. Tony was stinky—but Sweaty Lemonade Girl was no prize either. *Clearly,* he thought, *Sweaty Lemonade Girl has no idea how to run a business.*

Ernie tossed a few coins on the counter. "Put that one on me," he said.

Sweaty Lemonade Girl eyed the coins and begrudgingly poured a glass of lemonade for Tony. She put it on the counter and scooped up the change.

"Thanks, mister," the kid said, turning toward Ernie. "Name's Tony."

"Ernie, here. Pretty good with a shovel, kid," said Ernie.

"I try," said Tony with a shrug.

Ernie leaned in confidentially and lowered his voice so that Sweaty Lemonade Girl couldn't overhear. "I'm looking for somebody to dig a few holes," he said. "You interested?"

Tony looked both ways and back across the counter. Sweaty Lemonade Girl pursed her lips and arched her eyebrows as if she was suddenly all interested in Tony's business.

Tony turned his back to the counter and perched against his elbows. He tilted his head toward Ernie and answered, "Depends." He knocked back his lemonade, crumpled the cup, and chucked it over the counter.

"Hey!" Sweaty Lemonade Girl grumbled with annoyance. As she bent over to pick up the cup, Tony leaned in confidentially against Ernie and whispered, "What do I have to bury?"

Over the next week, Ernie had Tony and Dusty working like dogs on the empty lot. Tony hacked through the undergrowth with a huge pair of hedge clippers he had borrowed from his dad. Dusty spent the afternoon hauling all manner of debris to the curb.

When the shrubs and trees were clipped back, Tony showed up with his dad's Weedwacker and carefully cut the grass until it was as smooth as a golf course's. Ernie tried to take a crack at the Weedwacker himself, but Tony held him off.

"Forget it, Mr. Castellano," Tony said, "this is a job for a professional."

When the yard was finally cleaned up, they set about making improvements. And that was when Dusty went to town.

Dusty's first idea was to scavenge through the neighborhood for discarded plants and potted mums. He showed up with a red wagon full of wilted plants, mostly with dead blossoms.

Tony took one look at the wagon and said, "Who died?"

"I don't know about this, Dusty," said Ernie. "Those flowers look kind of ragged and pathetic."

"Give 'em time, Boss," Dusty insisted. "They'll look better in time."

Dusty replanted the flowers around the base of the trees. After a little sunlight and a little water, Ernie had to agree with Dusty. The flowers didn't look bad at all.

Pretty soon, they were all coming up with great ideas like that.

Tony had found a slightly trashed trellis in the alley and dragged it into the lot. "I figure, fix the broken slats with a couple nails, slap on a fresh coat of paint," Tony said, "it'll be like brand new."

And it pretty much was. When the paint had dried, Dusty tugged overgrown vines from the fence and laced them through the trellis, hoping they would grow.

As he was weaving the vines, Ernie arrived with a broken piano bench he'd found on the curb. He placed it below the trestle. "It'll be a place for quiet reflection," he said.

"That's just what I was thinking," Dusty agreed.

Ernie remembered an aluminum picnic table in the basement that they never used anymore. It had belonged to his mom before he was born. He and Tony carried the picnic table upstairs and hauled it down the alley. They positioned it on the back side of the lot and moved it five different times until Dusty decided that it was in the right spot.

Meanwhile, Dusty was scouring the neighborhood for big, flat rocks. He covered the picnic table with newspaper and spent the afternoon painting the rocks all sorts of different colors. "It's like painting Easter eggs," he said, "only much much bigger."

When Dusty was done, they laid the painted rocks in a winding trail across the lawn. It was backbreaking work—but after he put the last rock in place, Tony looked at Ernie and nodded in favor. Ernie smiled. "The place is looking good," he told Tony. "I tell you, that Dusty, he's got a million ideas."

For the crowning touch, Dusty climbed on Ernie's shoulders to crawl into the tallest tree on the lot. Clinging to the overhead branches, Dusty hung that wind chime he'd been working on. It was made out of those wire hangers, and he had added lots of discarded silverware, hammered flat.

Every time a breeze brushed through the tree, the wind chime clanked and clattered and sent a strange little tune into the air.

All in all, they had turned the old abandoned lot into a lovely little garden.

Only nobody knew.

Chapter Five

Cat Lady

The next word on Ernie's list of things to do was *clients*.

"You know, customers," he explained to Dusty. "We need to let people know we're open for business."

Dusty spent that day in art class designing a flyer for the business. He carefully drew a picture of a puppy with wings. In a halo above the puppy, Dusty wrote down the essential information about the business: LOSE A LOVED ONE? PET FUNERALS. 555-2001.

After school, Ernie, Dusty, and Tony canvassed the neighborhood on bicycles looking for clients. Tony poked flyers between the spokes on other kids' bikes. Dusty taped one to a skateboard.

Ernie stopped his bicycle outside a fenced-in yard. "Hang on!" he cried to Tony and Dusty. "I just struck the mother lode."

When Tony and Dusty arrived on the scene, Ernie pointed over the fence. Cats of all shapes and sizes lined the yard. Thirty, forty, fifty cats. Siamese cats, gray cats, calico cats, even a black cat or two. Tony and Dusty hustled beside Ernie to peer over the fence.

"Oh, no. Mr. Castellano," Tony warned, "I wouldn't go in there! That's Cat Lady's house!"

At the very mention of her name, Dusty yelped. "I'm not going near Cat Lady," he said shivering.

"Cat Lady?" Ernie asked. "Who's Cat Lady?"

"I heard she cries all night," said Dusty.

"I heard she sneaks into people's houses and steals kittens," Tony said with definite relish.

"In her mouth!" Dusty exclaimed.

Tony chortled fiendishly for dramatic effect. "And then she fattens up her cats and eats fat-cat stew!"

Ernie scoffed with disbelief. "Cat Lady? You scaredy-cats don't know a business opportunity when it's staring you in the face." With that, Ernie pushed through the gate.

Tony and Dusty were absolutely stunned.

Ernie crept across the yard toward a rustic cottage with a wraparound porch. Everywhere he turned, he saw cats. It seemed as if dozens were lining the

25

porch and windowsills. There were so many cats that Ernie couldn't resist counting.

"Eleven, twelve, thirteen, fourteen, fifteen . . . ," he said.

The top half of the front door swung open with a sharp creak. "Two hundred ninety-seven," a voice announced in a sarcastic tone.

Ernie jumped.

Cat Lady stood at the door with a fat cat cradled in her arms. "At last count," she added with a smile.

The sight of Cat Lady startled Ernie. Mostly because she had caught him by surprise. He was expecting to see an old hag, but Cat Lady was actually a young woman—certainly as young as Ms. Pringle or any of his substitute teachers. But Cat Lady wasn't dressed like a schoolteacher. She clutched her housecoat closed tight, as though she hadn't stepped outside in a few days. Her hair was bent into odd shapes from lounging on the sofa. She looked like she was having a bad day. Or a bad week. Maybe a bad month.

Ernie noticed that the fat cat in Cat Lady's arms was wearing a name tag on his collar. The name tag read: #62.

Cat Lady noticed that Ernie was reading the name tag and she smiled. But it wasn't the nicest smile.

"#62, see?" she snapped. "I number as many as I can, but those cats are quicker than you think. Especially the fat ones."

She shook the cat so Ernie could see just how fat he had gotten. Then she jabbed a finger at Ernie and said, "What do you want?"

Ernie flashed a smile and pulled out a flyer. "Ernie Castellano, ma'am," he said. "I'm opening a pet cemetery and thought you might need my services."

Cat Lady bristled, but Ernie pressed on. "As an introductory offer, we've got a bulk rate on any departed kitties you just might have lying around," he continued.

At that point, Cat Lady cut him off. She had heard enough. "Get off my property!" she barked. "I'm not handing my kitties over so you and your friends can wail and blubber and boo-hoo-hoo."

"What, you mean crying?" Ernie said—even as he thought to himself, *Crying, yeah, crying. I hadn't thought of that.*

Cat Lady cracked a kitchen towel in his direction. "Get out of here!" she said. "Get out or I'll sic the cats on you. Scram! Beat it!"

Ernie dropped a flyer on the porch and zigzagged past the cats in the yard. By the time he reached the fence, he was already thinking, *Crying. We need a crybaby! We need a crier for hire!*

From her front porch, Cat Lady watched as the boy left her yard. She continued to glower at him from a distance. "The nerve!" Cat Lady muttered to herself. "Knockin' on my door. Dreadful little brat." She smiled at Cat #62 in her arms and continued,

"I must not be as scary as I thought. Am I, kitty? Grrr. Grrrr."

Cat #62 jostled in her arms and turned in the other direction as if he had better things to do and she was holding him up.

Cat Lady thought, *I gotta stop talking to cats.*

Ernie pushed through the fence and onto the sidewalk. Tony flagged his arms like an umpire and called out, "Safe! Whew, Mr. Castellano, you're my new hero!"

Ernie looked left and right, but there was no sight of Dusty. "Where's Dusty?" he asked.

"Ran off," Tony said with a shrug. He jabbed a thumb in the direction of Cat Lady's house and mocked a shudder. "Said she's too scary. So. How'd it go?"

Ernie seemed distracted. He was already thumbing through his notebook for the last empty page. "What? Who? Cat Lady?" he asked. "Nah. She was nice."

"Nice?" Tony repeated, completely flabbergasted. He'd never heard anybody say that Cat Lady was nice before. Tony started to press for more information— but Ernie changed the subject.

"Hey, Tony," he said. "You ever cry?"

"You're kidding me, right?" Tony smirked and shuffled in place. "Castellano, you're cracking me up today."

"Yeah, I know, me neither," Ernie replied. "Still . . ."

Ernie found the last page of entries in his notebook and scratched his stub of a pencil through the words *boxes*, *holes*, and *clients*.

"So far so good, huh, Mr. Castellano?" Tony asked.

"Yeah, but still plenty of work to do," said Ernie.

He gripped the stub of a pencil tighter and added another word to the list.

Crybaby.

Chapter Six

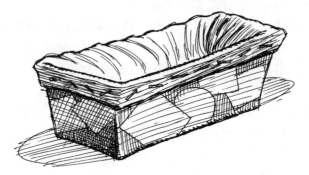

A Whole New Ernie

It looked as though Ernie finally had his business in place.

The cemetery was looking great, the customers were trickling in—and Ernie had become a whole new Ernie. He almost *looked* like a real businessman, wearing his dad's old sport coat with the sleeves rolled, standing on the top step of his back stoop and barking into a cell phone.

"Matt, Matt, Matt," he cried. "I do not gouge my customers! The price is ten dollars. . . . No, *ten* dollars. . . . The price is frozen, like Ben & Jerry's."

At that moment, a fence board swung back and Dusty stepped through the gap and into the yard. His overalls were covered in smudges of paint, and he was hauling his old-fashioned suitcase. From the sight of the shoe box tucked under Dusty's arm, Ernie knew that Dusty had finished the latest box—right on schedule. Good old reliable Dusty. He was worth his weight in gold.

"Hey, Boss," Dusty said with a short, brisk salute.

"Hey, Dusty," Ernie responded. "Gimme a minute." Ernie gestured toward the phone. Dusty nodded and promptly sat down on the stoop to wait out the call.

Ernie took a deep breath. He switched his voice to a gentler tone, like he was speaking to an unreliable child, and said, "Matt, Matt, do as I say. Tell Mom and Dad you're going to a movie, you need the popcorn, score the ten bucks, and give little Frisky the send-off he deserves."

Matt must have raised a little protest on the other end of the phone, because Ernie blustered as though he wouldn't hear it. Ernie had an answer for everything.

"Matt! Hit your parents for that new monster movie. The giant bug. I already saw it; you're not missing nothing."

Ernie smiled at Dusty and gestured that this would take only a moment longer. He was clearly gaining control of the situation.

"Good. . . . Good, Matt. . . . We'll see you tomorrow. . . . Good-bye. . . . Good-bye. . . . Bye-bye."

Ernie snapped the cell phone lid shut for dramatic effect. Suddenly it was just Ernie and Dusty in the yard.

"I'm gonna have an ulcer before I learn how to drive," Ernie groused as he tossed the phone into his coat pocket. He turned his attention to Dusty with a businesslike air. "Okay, Dusty. You got the box?"

"You're gonna love it, Boss." Dusty grinned. "It's a real beauty."

Dusty drew his arms from behind his back and presented the shoe box with a flourish. He whisked back the lid with flair, like a waiter in a fancy restaurant. "Voilà," said Dusty.

The shoe box was broad and deep and painted a dark purple. "I snagged the Michael Jordan high-tops box from some Dumpster behind the gym," Dusty explained. "Should be deep enough, I bet. And I spray-painted it purple 'cause I ran out of blue."

Ernie took the box into his hands and turned it over. The four sides were covered in photos clipped out of a magazine. "What are these pictures?" he asked.

"*National Geographic*," Dusty replied. He pointed to certain details. "That's a baby dinosaur egg, and the next one is a baby dinosaur when it's just been born."

"Hmm. Isn't that interesting." Ernie seemed impressed.

Dusty ran his hand across the interior of the

box. "And I lined the inside with this big, crazy scarf I found in my mom's closet."

"Very nice," said Ernie. "But," he hesitated, "isn't your mom going to miss that scarf?"

Dusty waved him aside with a dismissive gesture. "Not in a million years," he said. "My mom's a total pack rat. She's got closets and drawers full of this stuff. She'll never notice one crazy scarf is gone."

"And where this scarf's going, she's not gonna look," Ernie added with a snicker.

Dusty snickered too, although he wasn't exactly sure why. "Is the bunny here yet?" he asked.

Ernie referred to his notebook with a professional air and announced, "The deceased arrives with the client at a quarter to four."

Dusty dug the toe of his sneaker into the dirt and thought out loud, "Quarter to four. A quarter to four . . ."

Ernie snapped. "Three forty-five. The big hand on the nine, the little hand on the—"

"Three forty-five," Dusty interrupted. "Why didn't you say so? 'A quarter to four.'"

Ernie referred to his notebook and barreled onward. "Visitation from four till a quarter past. Funeral at four-fifteen," he said. "Burial to follow."

Dusty nodded. "So okay. You wanna pay me up front, or should I write out a bill?" he asked.

Ernie admired the way Dusty could cut to the chase when it came to business. "I can pay you up front," he answered, "but I need a bill for my records."

Dusty was one step ahead of him. He pulled a small pad from his hip pocket and a thick black crayon from his overalls. He crooked his leg up against the stoop, using his knee as a desk, and recited as he wrote, "'One Jurassic Bunny Box. Two seventy-five.'"

Ernie balked. "Two seventy-five? What happened to two dollars?"

Dusty instantly started to argue his case. He held his finger a lot. There was a thick Band-Aid wrapped all around the tip. "Boss, I got a paper cut doing this job," he argued. "I ruined my dad's magazine. This is no two-dollar job."

Ernie was rigid. "We said two dollars," he said.

Dusty thrust the box under Ernie's nose. "But Boss, look at that craftsmanship! Jurassic Bunny Box is right up there with the Star-Studded Cylinder for Sissy the Snake," Dusty said with a toothy smile. The Star-Studded Cylinder had been a big hit.

Ernie held firm. "Two dollars."

"But Boss! This is no two-dollar job. I ruined my dad's magazine. And I got a paper cut doing this job!"

"Two dollars."

"But this is *art*, Boss!" Dusty cried.

Ernie waved a dismissive hand. "Art schmart. We agreed on two dollars."

Dusty took a last-ditch effort. "Two fifty," he pleaded, fingering the scarf that lined the box.

"That scarf is like a Pucci original or something."

Ernie snatched the box out of Dusty's hands. "It's a dead bunny, Dusty. Dead bunnies don't know from Pucci. Two dollars. Going once, going twice. Going, going . . ."

Dusty knew when to cut his losses. "Okay, okay," he said as he held out his palm. "Two bucks."

Ernie whipped out his wallet to pay Dusty on the spot. He had a habit of fingering each dollar bill independently as he counted it off. "One, two . . . two dollars," he said, pressing the bills into Dusty's palm. Dusty pocketed the money in his overalls as Ernie stowed away his wallet.

"Say," Ernie added in a friendlier voice, "you wanna hang around for the services? I might need another usher."

Dusty wiped a smudge of paint off his nose and squinted at Ernie. "I did want to see that dead bunny," he admitted.

That was all Ernie needed to hear. "Come back at four," he said.

With that, Ernie hunched down over his notebook calculations with a pencil. Dusty nodded and waved a quick good-bye. He knew not to bug Ernie when he had business on his mind. Ernie was becoming a good friend, but when it came to business, Ernie was all business.

Dusty hauled his suitcase across the lot and swung open the fence board to sneak across the next yards back to his place.

Ernie entered the dollar amount of their trans-
action into his notebook as the fence board shut
with a loud *bang*.

Dang, he thought, *I forgot to ask Dusty*.

Ernie snapped his fingers and jumped to his
feet.

"Hey, Dusty," he hollered. "Hang on a minute!"

Dusty's head appeared over the top of the
fence. He wobbled a bit, so Ernie could tell that he
must be standing on top of his suitcase.

"What's up, Boss?" he asked.

Ernie dropped his hands, since it was obvious
he didn't have to holler. "Hey, Dusty," he said. "You
know anybody who can cry?"

Chapter Seven

Somebody Who Can Cry

There's no rule that says that a girl in red high-top sneakers is absolutely a tomboy. Generalizations like that don't really hold up.

But it is true that certain tomboys believe that red high-top sneakers bring good luck. At least, that's what Swimming Pool believed. And she was a tomboy with a pair of red high-top sneakers.

Swimming Pool had begged her parents to give her the shoes for her eleventh birthday. They were still pretty new, but they didn't look all that new. They were covered in graffiti. The laces were a wreck. The soles were all worn out because Swimming Pool wore them all the time.

She wore them when she was at church and she wore them when she was at school. They were especially good for kicking a soda can, hopping through a double Dutch, jumping a curb on a skateboard, and stamping at lizards.

Swimming Pool told people she wore red high-top sneakers because they were so comfortable—but secretly Swimming Pool believed the sneakers brought good luck. Which was why Swimming Pool thought it was probably a good idea to wear her sneakers to this job interview that Dusty told her about.

And of course, those red high-tops were the first thing that Ernie noticed about the girl that Dusty had recommended for the job. *Red high-top sneakers?* thought Ernie. He rumpled his lip. Clearly Ernie didn't think the red high-tops were such a good idea.

Ernie had been relieved, of course, when Dusty said he knew somebody who could cry. But Ernie was expecting a little second-grade waif. Some shy petunia or shrinking violet. Somebody a lot more demure. Instead, he was looking down his steps at one of the toughest little tomboys he'd ever seen.

Besides the sneakers, Swimming Pool wore loose hand-me-down overalls. Her baseball cap was twisted around backward. Every inch was covered with dirt and grass stains. It looked like she had just raced off the sandlot from a softball game—which, in fact, she had.

Swimming Pool didn't flinch as Ernie scrutinized her from above. She tilted her head to one side, crossed her arms, and stared right back at Ernie, not intimidated in the least.

Ernie broke the awkward silence. "So," he said, "the Dust Man says you can cry."

The tomboy shrugged. "Been known to shed a few."

"Give me a for instance."

She bent down and pulled up her pant leg to show off a large scab on her left knee. "Skinned my knee in Little League," she said. "Cracked the cap right on home plate. Umpire said he *heard* it crack. Yeah, I cried a little."

Ernie nodded coolly. "What else," he said.

The tomboy gestured toward her ear. "Got kicked in the head in Pee-Wee Soccer," she said. "Sure, I cried. It was Pee-Wee Soccer. I was still little."

"Keep going," Ernie said with a poker face.

The tomboy sighed heavily and winced like she was thinking hard. Then she snapped her fingers and launched into the story. "My brother's Rollerblades. Coming off a whip. Landed on the heel of my palm and busted this bone right here. You ever break a bone?"

"Never been so lucky," Ernie muttered.

The tomboy spoke with authority. "First you throw up, and then you go pale, and then it was still hurting and everybody was yelling, so . . . yeah, I cried a bit."

Ernie flinched at the description. He tapped his pencil against his notebook and adjusted his glasses on his nose. "Anything else?" he asked.

"Let's see," the girl muttered. "Knee, elbow, head, this bone here." She shrugged her shoulders and shoved her hands in her pockets. "Nope. Nothing else."

Ernie nodded two or three times. He stood up on the top step of the stoop and thought briefly before speaking. He clasped his hands over his mouth. He took off his glasses and pinched the crown of his nose.

"Look. My clients want to hear sadness. They don't want to hear your pain. Ever cry 'cause you were just sad or scared and stuff?"

The tomboy scoffed gently, as though Ernie had just made a joke. "You got the wrong girl," she said.

Ernie pressed further. "Never had a pet that died, for instance?"

"Dad won't let us have pets. He's allergic to the hair."

"'Allergic to the hair,' eh? What about a fish? A bird? A turtle?"

"Mom won't put up with the smell."

"'Mom won't put up with the smell.' Nothing hairy, nothing smelly." No pets in that household at all. He sat back on the stoop and scrutinized the tomboy below. "So," he said with an air of confusion. "What am I gonna do with you?"

The cell phone in his pocket began to ring.

"Excuse me a moment," Ernie offered. He

pulled the phone out of his jacket, popped open the cover, raised the antenna, and spoke with great authority. "It's Ernie," he barked. "You got him."

The tomboy moved to one side to give Ernie some privacy, but she couldn't help eavesdropping a little bit.

"Matt!" Ernie cried. "Got you and Frisky down for tomorrow at eleven. It's frozen! Like Ben & Jerry's! Everything's set."

The squawking that came through the phone suggested that Matt was not a happy camper. Ernie furrowed his brow but composed himself and continued. "Matt, I thought we already agreed on this. The price is ten dollars."

Swimming Pool arched an eyebrow. *Wow*, she thought, *ten dollars!* Where Swimming Pool came from, ten dollars was a lot of money.

Ernie was quickly working the situation to his advantage. "Well, you think about it, but don't think too long," Ernie said into the phone. "Did you put Frisky in the freezer? . . . Do what I say. You'll thank me later. . . . It's hard, I know."

He moved his face closer to the mouthpiece and spoke in reassuring tones. "Remember that little face on Frisky, those cute little paws, that cute little . . . ," Ernie cooed into the telephone, as though he was calming a child. He issued a short little "awwww."

Once he had Matt hooked with the sentiment, Ernie went for the jugular. "Yeah," he snarled.

41

"Just remember that little face and think about the send-off Frisky's gonna get for less than ten dollars."

Swimming Pool arched another eyebrow. *Wow*, she thought, *this kid plays hard ball.*

Matt must have said okay, because Ernie hustled him off the phone. "Pleasure doing business with you, Matt," he said, "Okay, bye. . . . Okay, bye. . . . Okay, bye. . . . Okay, bye."

Ernie snapped the phone shut and turned back to the tomboy so quickly that it startled her.

"Okay, back to you," he said. "Tell me something sad."

"Ha. No. Forget it."

Ernie descended the steps until he was standing beside her. "Look," he said. "I'm offering you a buck fifty to work one half hour. If I'm paying you a buck fifty, I wanna hear something sad."

Swimming Pool hedged a moment and stubbed the toe of her sneaker in the dirt around the bottom step before speaking. "My brother Rick left home once," she said. "That was sad."

"That make you cry?"

Swimming Pool twisted her head and reflexively clenched a fist. "None of your business," she grumbled.

Ernie saw the fist and backed off. He took three long steps backward into the center of his yard. "Look," he said, "I've got a yardful of bereaved bunny owner coming in about a half an hour. I need someone who's gonna cry for that dead bunny like it was her best friend."

"I can cry," Swimming Pool offered. "Watch me. I can fake it."

"I'm not interested in faking it," Ernie protested. "I run a clean show; my clients expect quality. If you're not gonna be able to pump out the real McCoy, I don't need you hogging space around the hole. I get plenty of onlookers."

"Okay, okay," Swimming Pool said, shaking her hands to clear the air. "I'll cry, I'll cry. It's no big deal."

"Okay then. Now you're talking," Ernie said.

Swimming Pool smiled with a bit of relief.

"But is that what you're planning to wear?" Ernie continued, giving Swimming Pool's outfit the once-over.

Swimming Pool looked down at her perfectly good jeans. "What's wrong with it?"

"Get yourself a dress," Ernie snapped. "And while you're at it"—he opened his notebook, licked the tip of his pencil, and poised it over the paper—"you got a name?"

Swimming Pool sighed. *Here it comes*, she thought. She looked at Ernie with a blank expression and said flatly, "Swimming Pool."

"Swimming Pool?" asked Ernie, not believing his ears.

That was exactly the reaction that Swimming Pool had come to expect. Ernie shook his head as though this name just wouldn't do at all. "Gonna have to get a better name than Swimming Pool," he said. "How about a normal name? Like Jennifer or Susan or Nancy."

Swimming Pool considered her situation for a moment—and then she hopped off the stoop and waved good-bye. "See you later," she said. "This isn't working for me. What say we cut our losses and I vamoose."

Ernie balked. "I thought you wanted to work!"

Swimming Pool was already scaling the fence. She stopped as she straddled the top to turn back. "Oh, I did," she said. "But mostly I wanted the buck fifty. Only—the name, the dress, the boo-hoo-hoo? We all got our limits!"

Ernie wanted to argue, but all he managed to say was, "Swimming Pool!"

And Swimming Pool was gone.

Chapter Eight

That Ding-dang Dress

*S*wimming Pool rode her bike up the driveway and sailed into the open garage. She hopped off the bike and let it keep on rolling until it crashed against all her brothers' bikes, stacked against the wall.

Score, she thought, *a direct hit.*

Swimming Pool did a little victory dance and acknowledged the cheering crowds. What she needed now was a drink.

The refrigerator in the garage was buried behind a couple heaps of laundry. Swimming Pool climbed over the mounds in front of the washer and dryer, flinging clothes right and left. She yanked open the refrigerator door. There was a jug of orange juice inside, but Swimming Pool stopped in her tracks.

I don't have a glass, she thought.

It was strictly against house rules to drink the orange juice straight from the jug. If her dad caught them drinking from the jug, he went berserk. *But I can't help it*, Swimming Pool thought. *It's hot and I'm thirsty, and besides, nobody's looking.*

She twisted her baseball cap backward and began to swig the juice straight from the bottle, splashing some down the front of her overalls. She stopped to catch her breath, wiped her chin, and went for another healthy swig.

This time, however, the swig was interrupted by the sound of shouting and doors slamming inside the house. Swimming Pool couldn't make out what all the yelling was about, except that both sides were hopping mad and nobody was giving in.

She could hear her brothers run upstairs, snickering and cackling. And she could hear her brother Rick—clear as a bell. Only she didn't like what she heard from Rick. What Rick was shouting was, "Yeah, well, I'm outta here! For good!"

A moment later, Rick stormed into the garage. He caught Swimming Pool at the open refrigerator with the jug of orange juice in her hand and a guilty expression on her face. She wiped her mouth and tossed the jug into the fridge.

"Don't tell Mom and Dad," Swimming Pool said, referring to the orange juice. They had already gotten on her case a couple times.

"Mom and Dad?" Rick scoffed. "Don't worry.

46

I'm never talking to them ever again! I'm moving out! Ridiculous house, ridiculous rules. I'm sick of it!"

Rick pulled a pair of drumsticks out of his hip pocket and began drumming angrily against the side of the dryer.

Swimming Pool thought Rick was the coolest kid in the world. And besides being her brother, Rick was almost like her best friend. They fought, of course, but they always got along, too. Swimming Pool felt she pretty much knew Rick inside and out. It was weird.

But Rick and his parents could never seem to get along. Rick was angry all the time—and he was always getting into fights with his brothers. It was kind of a problem in the house. Although Rick had announced before that he was running away, Swimming Pool didn't like the sound of it this time. Rick had never actually said it as though he really meant it.

"You're running away?" she asked.

"Nuh-uh," Rick snapped. "I'm not running away. I'm already outta here! I am gone. I am so gone!"

He grabbed a laundry basket from near the dryer and began to stuff it with T-shirts, under-wear, and jeans. Swimming Pool cringed. She knew that tone in Rick's voice. It was the same tone he'd used with her parents. She backed off fast, muttering her frustration under her breath.

Rick felt like a jerk. He hadn't meant to snap at Swimming Pool. She wasn't the problem. "Hey," he said, softening, "sorry. It's not your fault."

"I know it's not my fault. I know it's not my fault," Swimming Pool repeated.

"Hey, it's not my fault either," said Rick.

"Then whose fault is it?" Swimming Pool demanded.

Rick glared at her as though his head would explode. He grabbed the laundry basket under his arm and turned toward the door.

"Rick. Don't go," Swimming Pool begged. "You're the only brother I like. You're the only brother who doesn't hold me down and rub gum in my hair. You know how mean they are. Rick, if you leave, I'm gonna be all alone."

Rick grunted and grimaced. It was hard to listen to Swimming Pool when she got upset. He stowed away his drumsticks and reached under her arms to scoop her up.

"Come on. Don't cry," Rick said.

"I'm not! Quit it!" Swimming Pool snapped harshly. Her baseball cap fell off as Rick lifted her onto the washer. He stooped down to pick it up and put it back on her head. "Water Wiggle, we're a team, right?"

Rick was always thinking up other nicknames for her instead of "Swimming Pool." No matter how much she asked him to stop it, he never did. And truth be told, Swimming Pool kind of liked it.

"We stick together," Rick continued. "Thick and thin."

"Right," Swimming Pool scoffed. "That's why I was counting on you to stick up for me and teach me stuff. You said we were a team. You said we'd stick together. Thick and thin. So where are you going? What's going on? Nobody tells me nothing."

Swimming Pool flopped down on a pile of rumpled towels and wrapped her arms around her chest. She didn't mean to sulk. She didn't mean to cry, either. She was just tired of thinking about it. She stuck out her lower lip and refused to look Rick in the eye.

Rick felt like a total heel. He moved in carefully and nudged Swimming Pool's shoulder with a gentle fist, kind of solemn and serious for a moment.

"I'm not going to live here anymore, Swimming Pool. I am moving out. But you gotta promise me. No tears. You're tough, remember? Tough like me."

Swimming Pool pouted and repeated the words: "I'm tough. I'm tough."

"It won't be so bad," Rick said, trying to make light of the situation.

"How do you know? You're not going to be around!"

Rick was getting frustrated with the whole good-bye. "It's just gonna be what it is," he mumbled. "Don't be going on about it." He went back to stuffing the laundry basket full of clothes.

Swimming Pool softened. If Rick was actually moving out of the house, where was he going to go? She went ahead and asked him. "Where are you

49

going to live? Where are you going to sleep?"

"I dunno," Rick muttered. "I haven't gotten to that part yet. I'll have to get a job, I guess. But don't you worry. I'll get by."

Swimming Pool looked up. It was hard to think of Rick with a job. He had a hard enough time getting along with the family. And she couldn't remember a day when Rick had actually done his share of the household chores.

Besides, Rick was always diving into the deep end before he'd figured things out. Swimming Pool was much better at planning ahead than Rick—but that's just the way he was.

With a sense of purpose, Swimming Pool got to her feet on top of the washer. She turned around, opened the cupboard, and pulled out a coffee can from its hiding place. She shook the can and it rattled with coins. That got Rick's attention.

Swimming Pool looked down at him. "You're gonna need money," she said.

"I'm not taking your money, Baby Bubble. Besides, I'm gonna need more money than that."

"I've got *quarters*," Swimming Pool argued.

"I need more than quarters and I'm not taking your money!" Rick argued back.

"Fine! Be that way!" Swimming Pool snapped.

She sulked and he grunted. This was usually the way it went with them when Swimming Pool and Rick fought. A total breakdown of communication.

But this time, Rick felt bad right away. He

didn't want his good-bye to go like this—not with another fight. He pulled the drumsticks out of his hip pocket and tapped lightly on Swimming Pool's baseball cap. Swimming Pool jerked but she didn't pull away.

"Quit," she said.

Rick leaned in a little closer and nudged her playfully with his elbow. "Mmmmmmmmmarco . . . ," he said.

Swimming Pool smirked but did not respond.

"Come on, say it!" he said sweetly. "Mmmmmarco . . .'"

It was this silly game they played around the house. More of a private joke, really. It was that game that kids play in the pool in the summertime—except Rick and Swimming Pool played it all year long on dry land.

But Swimming Pool wasn't through sulking, so she didn't want to play. "I'm not playing that game anymore," Swimming Pool answered. "Quit it!"

Rick poked her with a drumstick. "Come on, say it," he teased. "Mmmmmarco. Marco . . ." He pinched Swimming Pool playfully on the leg.

When Rick teased her, Swimming Pool got so exasperated she didn't know whether to punch him or cry. But even as she was balling up a knuckle sandwich to clomp him on the head, they heard more shouting from the house.

Rick stiffened. "I better run," he said. "I'll come back for my drums. Don't tell Dad you saw me."

"As if I would," Swimming Pool muttered.

"Just don't!" Rick said. He grabbed a laundry basket brimming with clothes and ran down the driveway. He circled his old beat-up green van, which was parked along the curb. Swimming Pool heard the driver's door open on the other side.

Swimming Pool ran onto the driveway just as the car engine sprang to life. "Rick!" she called out, but too late for him to hear.

The dirty green van let out a rumble and a gust of exhaust. Swimming Pool winced as the van kicked into gear. It lurched away from the curb and drove off down the street.

Swimming Pool stood in the center of the road to watch as Rick drove away. She waved frantically, but she had no idea whether Rick was even looking in the rearview mirror.

She tried to yell above the rumble of the van. "Polo!" she cried. "Marco Polo!" But it was too late. Rick was gone.

Swimming Pool walked back into the garage. What could she do? She had to help Rick. But how?

Then it occurred to her. "That job," she said to herself. "That ding-dang job with the dress." She started clawing through the clothes in front of the washer. "Where's that ding-dang dress I had to wear?"

Swimming Pool grabbed one of her brothers' hockey shirts from a laundry basket and held it up to her shoulders. It had NORTHSIDE VIKINGS written on it and a big number twenty-three but Swimming Pool figured it might work as a dress if she cinched it with a belt. She held it with one hand and sashayed from side to side, trying to get the hockey shirt to swing like a dress. *Nah,* she thought as she balled up the shirt and tossed it at the basket. A solid dunk. Two points.

She started another little victory dance, but her feet got knotted up. She looked down and saw that she was standing on it. That awful little-girl dress her mom had made her wear to her aunt's wedding. A dreadful purple thing with puffy sleeves, pleats, and crisscross smocking. At the time, Swimming Pool had said, "Never again." Today, though, the dress was just what she had in mind. She scooped it up and shook it out. "This ought to do just fine."

She hauled the dress over her head, fumbling when she missed the neck hole. For a moment, she was trapped inside all that purple. But with a yank and a tug, Swimming Pool's head popped through the collar.

I'm gonna wear this dress, she thought. *I'm gonna wear this dress and I'm gonna nail that job.*

Chapter Nine

A Garage Like Home

$\mathcal{D}$**usty's parents used** the toolshed for rusted bikes, lawn furniture, and old newspapers heaped in recycling bins. To them, it was a storeroom.

To Dusty, the toolshed was an artist's studio. It was quiet. And it had a good overhead light and a big worktable. Most kids would have preferred fresh air and a wide-open field to being cooped up inside a wooden shed. But this was how Dusty liked to work. Tinkering away in a quiet, cool corner.

He popped the latches on his old suitcase and it sprang open on top of the workbench. Dusty kept the suitcase fairly bulging with crayons, Styrofoam, cardboard, pie tins, paint, glue, feathers, pipe cleaners, and scraps of wild, mismatched fabric. When it came to art supplies, Dusty was a pack rat and everything was up for grabs.

Dusty selected a tube of paint and a nice fat paintbrush and began dabbing the final touches on a new project that involved a milk carton and a lot of spangles.

The door burst open and sunlight filled the toolshed. Dusty squinted into the glare and saw Ernie swinging on the door.

"What have you gotten me into, Dusty?" Ernie barked.

Dusty recognized the tone. Ernie was in a royal bad mood.

"She walked!" Ernie huffed as he squeezed into the toolshed. "I hadn't even hired her yet, and she walked!"

"You mean Swimming Pool, Boss?"

Ernie sat on top of the workbench, flung his arms, and hollered, "That little tomboy had me totally bamboozled!"

"That's too bad, Boss." Dusty shrugged. "I had a good feeling about Swimming Pool."

"And what's with that name, anyway?" Ernie snapped. "Swimming Pool?"

Dusty knew the whole story. It was actually a really good one. "Seven brothers. Swimming Pool's the baby. Mom's pregnant with Swimming Pool and everybody's like, 'What's it gonna be?' Mom says, 'A little *girl* would be nice.' But the brothers are like, 'A little girl? We'd rather have a *swimming pool!*'"

Dusty thrust his fists in the air and chanted like a football player, "Swim-ming *Pool!* Swim-ming *Pool!*"

He dropped his fists and shrugged. "It's been Swimming Pool ever since."

End of story. Dusty went back to work.

Ernie wasn't so very impressed.

"Well, it looks like Swimming Pool wasn't interested in being our crier. We got a funeral scheduled in twenty minutes and I still don't have a crybaby."

"But business is picking up, huh, Boss?" Dusty enthused, trying to concentrate on the positive side.

Ernie groaned with exasperation and rolled over on the workbench. In the process, he knocked into the new project that Dusty had been working on. It was a milk carton strung with shiny pop-tops along the sides. Ernie held the carton aloft. "What's this?" he asked.

"A Crystal Capsule for Kiwi's Canary," Dusty announced with his usual flourish.

"Excellent," Ernie said. "Only Kiwi's canary isn't dead."

"Not *yet*," Dusty observed. "But she was looking mighty peaked last time I stopped by."

"Is that right?"

Dusty shrugged. "Just staying ahead of the demand."

Ernie smirked. "You're good. You're very good."

"And it'll cost you two fifty," Dusty added—with emphasis on the fifty cents.

Ernie arched an eyebrow. Sometimes he had to give Dusty credit. "You're learning fast," he remarked.

"Speaking of which," Ernie continued with

annoyance, "Matt the Brat called to confirm the services and dicker over price. I told him the price is frozen like Ben & Jerry's—and to keep little Frisky on ice."

"Never liked that cat anyway," Dusty muttered.

"Me, neither," Ernie grunted. "You finish the box for Frisky?"

Dusty reached into his old suitcase and carefully raised an object with both hands. It was an oatmeal container painted with red and white stripes and rigged with a Frisbee like the brim on a hat.

"Cat in the Hat for Matt's Dead Cat," Dusty announced with a flourish.

"Perfect!" Ernie cried. "You're a genius." He sat on the edge of the workbench and reached up to pinch the muscles in his neck. "I tell you," he said, "I'm gonna have to take up the skateboard again. I'm carrying too much stress."

"Say, Boss," Dusty offered, "what say we knock off early tonight and catch a Slurpee down at the minimart?"

"Can't," Ernie said with a surly edge. "Gotta walk Mister Doggie. Dad's working a double, so guess who gets to walk it? When you gotta go, you gotta go."

"You could just tie Mister Doggie up in the garden," Dusty suggested. "There's plenty of yard."

"No can do," Ernie said. "Mister Doggie is 'too little for the big, bad world.' Too little even to run around." He reached to pop the latches on the suitcase open and shut a few times. "Besides," he said with a shrug, "it's just as well. He'd only dig up the clientele."

Ernie flipped his notebook open and ran through the checklist. "The Jurassic Bunny Box is done; we're all set for Frisky tomorrow. Now if only I could get a crybaby. What's a funeral without a crybaby?"

At that crucial moment, Dusty happened to sneeze. The dust in the toolshed was something of a problem. Dusty expected to hear Ernie say "gesundheit," but when he looked up, Ernie was just staring at him.

"What?" Dusty asked. He reached for a tissue and blew his nose. When he looked up again, Ernie was still looking at him.

"What?" Dusty asked again, with a little annoyance.

"I just found my crybaby," Ernie said, looking straight at Dusty.

"Boss, no! I can't!" Dusty cried.

"What d'you mean?" Ernie argued. "You were practically crying when I met you. Look, I'll pay extra! And if you have trouble, I'll give you a pinch."

"But Boss!" Dusty protested, desperate to get out of this situation with any dignity.

Chapter Ten

Chester Playboy Bunny

A light drizzle was falling as the sad but stately funeral procession entered the renovated cemetery lot. The mourners were all dressed in their Sunday best or their party clothes. Ernie had insisted that his clients and their guests wear their best clothes to these events out of respect for the departed.

The procession was led by Betty, the bereaved bunny owner—and she was a wreck. Betty huddled beneath sunglasses and a big old hat. Friends had to hold her up by the elbows as she hobbled along in her mother's pumps. She cradled a big box of bright yellow tissues. And every time she issued a big, dramatic sob, Betty threw a tissue into the air to waft to the ground behind her. Betty was quite a sight.

Two pallbearers followed Betty, carrying the Jurassic Bunny Box. Then came a fairly decent size crowd of sympathetic mourners. Many more than Ernie had expected. At the rear of the procession came Tony, dragging his great, big shovel against the ground.

Dusty stood at the gate to the cemetery, nodding solemnly as each kid arrived. He swept his arm out to gesture them to continue into the yard. Everyone was really quiet and grim. Dusty was careful to hold the old gate open so that it wouldn't bonk any of the mourners in the head.

Ernie stood in the center of the lawn, wearing one of Red's neckties and a pensive air. He nodded sympathetically and gestured the arriving mourners to stand in various spots about the yard. Betty stood on the far side of the grave site, just across from Ernie. Ernie made eye contact with her and winced sympathetically. He gave a little nod, and Betty offered a brave smile before she went back to her sniffles and sobs.

When all the mourners were assembled, Dusty left his position at the gate and walked slowly to Ernie's side.

"Okay, hit it, Dusty," Ernie said under his breath. "Turn on those tears."

"I can't do this, Boss," Dusty muttered helplessly.

"The big boo-hoo, Dusty. I need it now," Ernie urged with a nudge. "Don't make me stand out there and give a eulogy. You know I'm lousy at public speaking."

"Boss, I can't. You're embarrassing me," Dusty whined.

"You'll be crying when I fire you," Ernie warned. "Let's see some tears."

After a few moments of awkward silence, Ernie had no choice but to step forward and launch into a few words to commemorate the event. It was a really clumsy attempt at a eulogy.

All eyes were on Ernie. He cleared his throat and adjusted his tie. "Ahem," he declared, spreading his arms open wide. "Beloved Dearly."

At the sound of his voice, the mourners tilted their heads with thoughtful concern. *So far so good,* thought Ernie.

Ernie opened his mouth and tried to think of something to say. It was a false start because nothing was really coming to mind.

As if to rescue him from the moment, a rustle rose among the congregation. Tony was pushing through the crowd with his great big shovel. He stepped across the grave site, nearly clocking Betty with the shovel. When he reached Ernie, Tony extended his palm.

"Tony," Ernie said, slightly flustered. "What'd I say? Twenty-five cents?"

"Hey!" snapped Tony. "You said *fifty.*"

Ernie groped in his pockets for loose change. "Okay, okay," he groused, "two quarters. Start digging."

Tony pocketed the quarters and stepped before

61

the line of mourners. He started digging right in their midst. Every now and then, a scoop of dirt went flying through the air.

Ernie resumed his eulogy. "Ahem. Where was I?" he said.

"Beloved Dearly," the mourners answered in unison.

Ernie cleared his throat one more time and clumsily began his eulogy.

"We gather today to remember a truly great rabbit," Ernie said. That sounded good. "A rabbit among rabbits," he added. He let his gaze pause thoughtfully on the crowd before gently enunciating the name of the deceased. "Chester Playboy Bunny."

Betty lifted her head from a yellow tissue to utter a squeak and a sniffle. Her friends murmured sympathy and nodded their heads.

Ernie glanced back—but there was not a peep from Dusty. Dusty seemed to be taking a break from the action and was taking in the sights and sounds of the funeral. Ernie glared in his direction as he intoned to the congregation, "At moments like this, tears must be shed. At moments like this, we should be *sobbing!*"

At that moment, at the other end of the alley, Swimming Pool was charging at a breakneck pace in her red high-top sneakers and that awful purple dress. She vaulted over a garbage can, dodged a clothesline, ducked under a window, trashed a hedge, and scrambled over the old fence surrounding that empty lot opposite Dusty's.

So just as Ernie was saying "we should be *sobbing*," the fence around the lot began to rattle and shake. It was almost scary. And before the kids could figure out what was going on, Swimming Pool barreled into their midst.

Of course, suddenly all eyes were on Swimming Pool. No one had expected to see her at Chester Playboy's funeral. And on top of that, Swimming Pool was wearing a dress. Granted, it was a strange dress. It was all wrinkled purple taffeta, and not so much poofy as it was scrunched on one side. Swimming Pool had tried to tie the bow in back, but it basically turned out a knot.

Swimming Pool waved at Ernie, then she waved to Dusty, and then she gave a wave to Betty. After that, she bent over and panted like a dog. "Sorry," she said, "I'm totally out of breath." With another surge of energy, Swimming Pool took her position beside Dusty, clenched her arms, and shoved her lower lip out like she was the sergeant at arms.

Ernie bugged his eyes out at Dusty. It was a look that said, "What have you gotten me into here, Dusty?" Dusty flinched helplessly. Swimming Pool had shown up—but it was still anybody's guess as to whether she was going to cry.

"Swimming Pool," Dusty muttered, "I thought you ditched."

Swimming Pool shrugged. "What can I say? I need the dough."

Ernie excused himself briefly from the congregation and turned toward Swimming Pool. "So," Ernie said, "decided to join us, Swimming Pool?"

"Just get on with it, wise guy," she said.

Chapter Eleven

Poor Betty

Ernie turned back to face Betty and the entire congregation. "Beloved Dearly," he intoned again with great authority.

Swimming Pool nudged Dusty. "'Beloved Dearly'?" she rasped in a rough whisper. "Hasn't he got that backward?"

"*You* tell him," Dusty muttered. Then Dusty leaned over to cup his hand around Swimming Pool's ear. "Hey, Swimming Pool," he whispered. "You gonna be okay with this? I mean, are you gonna be able to cry?"

"Don't talk to me about that," Swimming Pool snapped. "I'm concentrating."

Of course, Ernie still had no idea what to say in a eulogy for a rabbit. "Chester Playboy Bunny," Ernie repeated, riffing nervously on the name of that dead bunny. "Some days he was Chester. Some days he was Playboy."

As the congregation began to nod and coo again, Ernie pivoted to hiss behind him, "*Swimming Pool! I need those tears!*"

Dusty turned toward her. "Excuse me," he said with extreme politeness, "but I believe you are supposed to be crying about now."

Swimming Pool rolled her eyes. "I'm working on it. Don't bug me!"

Swimming Pool tried bracing her index finger with her other hand—and poking herself in the eye. It hurt a little. But still not enough to make her cry.

Swimming Pool turned her fist into a knuckle sandwich and popped herself hard in the shoulder. It hurt, but not enough to make her cry. *Oh, well,* she thought.

By this point, Ernie's eulogy was coming out in awkward little dribs and drabs—and the improvisation was starting to show. "I never had the pleasure of seeing Chester Playboy hop through the park," Ernie blustered, "although I'm told Betty often took him there. To . . . hop about . . . like bunnies do."

A few of the kids grumbled, like "What the heck is he talking about?"

"But the Chester Playboy *I* remember," Ernie carried on with rambling vigor, "is the funny little rabbit who used to wiggle his nose through the holes of his cage. Who used to tug at a carrot—and didn't much like it if you tried to fool him with a finger."

"That's the truth," one mourner observed.

"He bit me once," said another. "It was so cute."

Some mourners were still nodding sympathetically. But others were getting skeptical. Ernie glanced desperately at Swimming Pool—but still not a peep.

"Swimming Pool," Dusty pleaded, "he's dying out there."

Swimming Pool shook her fist in Dusty's face. "Keep bugging me and you're gonna get a black eye," she warned.

Ernie was really winging it now. "Some say Chester Playboy died from the pesticide Mrs. Marshman puts on her stupid begonias. And I don't know. Maybe that's true. But I prefer to think that Chester Playboy died of a *broken heart*."

Betty issued another heavy sob.

Swimming Pool tried holding her eyelids open wide between her index finger and thumb until her eyes bulged like a bullfrog's. Still nothing.

"Because Chester Playboy *knew* Betty was going away for spring break—and who was gonna feed him?" Ernie asked with a slight tremor in his voice.

Swimming Pool stuck her tongue out and clamped down on it with her teeth. That hurt plenty. But still no tears.

"Who was gonna pet poor Chester Playboy?" Ernie rambled on. "Blow little kisses at his pink little nose?" Ernie paused for dramatic effect and observed the faces of the congregation. "It's a sad fact," he said, "but Chester Playboy was all alone."

The congregation shifted uneasily. "What?" someone asked delicately, even though she had heard Ernie quite clearly.

"I can't believe he just said that," one mourner mumbled to another.

"Was that remark entirely appropriate?" asked another. "Betty loved that bunny."

"How uncouth," another mourner remarked as the rumble of disapproval rolled through the congregation.

Swimming Pool bent her thumb back until it almost reached her arm. That really hurt plenty. But still no tears. She grunted with exasperation and went to work on the opposite thumb.

Meanwhile, Betty lowered her sunglasses to glower at Ernie. Suddenly the funeral was not going so well.

Ernie was desperate and Dusty was desperate for him. "Swimming Pool!" Dusty pleaded. "Hurry up and cry or something."

Swimming Pool was stomping on one foot with the heel of the other. "Nothing's coming up!" she blurted out, just about ready to admit defeat.

"I could pinch you real hard," Dusty offered.

"You want that black eye?" Swimming Pool barked.

Meanwhile, Ernie blustered and backpedaled

in his eulogy, trying to cover his gaffe and cut his losses. "Not that Betty meant to break her bunny's heart and send him off to bunny heaven, but because . . ."

Swimming Pool twisted her ears until they were red. She tugged her hair by the handful. Nothing was making her cry. Nothing, nothing.

"Think of *something sad*, Swimming Pool," Dusty suggested.

"I tried that!" she said with irritation.

By this point, Ernie was a sinking ship. "But we all have to go away sometimes," he ventured feebly, "and naturally our bunny rabbits are going to miss getting *fed*."

Ouch. The congregation audibly groaned. Ernie fidgeted in despair. That was it. He had mentioned the unmentionable. The whole neighborhood knew that Betty had left for a week at her cousin's beach house without leaving enough celery for Chester Playboy.

"He did not just say what I think he said."

"He should have stopped while he was ahead."

"Look! Betty's face is turning red!"

Everyone agreed that Betty must feel just awful.

Desperately, Dusty took a shot at rescuing the situation. He stepped forward and flung his arms to the air. "Boo-hoo!" he cried with deliberate drama. "Boo-hoo-hoo-hoo-hoo!"

There was a hushed moment of silence. The

congregation studied Dusty as though he had just gone crazy. Dusty hedged, skulked, and slunk away behind Swimming Pool.

"That was pathetic," he mumbled.

Chapter Twelve

The Wail

In a valiant effort, Ernie blustered into one last grand final sentence, hoping it would bring some kind of closure to his eulogy.

"And when the loved ones you love leave you behind," he began, "and you don't know where they're going but they're not coming back and you don't know why and nobody tells you nothing—and your heart is kind of breaking . . ."

Ernie and Dusty were too distracted to notice. And the entire congregation was too distracted to notice. But Swimming Pool's ears perked at this part of Ernie's eulogy.

She was hearing Ernie loud and clear. And everything Ernie said reminded her of her brother Rick.

It was all true. Rick was gone. And she didn't

know where Rick was going. And nobody told her nothing. And her heart was kind of breaking. Despite herself, Swimming Pool let out a peep.

"Eep!" It was more like that.

She caught herself gaping at the sound. As soon as the peep had popped out of her mouth, Swimming Pool clamped her hands over her face. Swimming Pool was aghast. *Where did that come from?* she wondered. *Uh-oh. If I start to cry now, I'm never going to stop.*

By then, of course, Betty was wailing. She was hysterical. She was inconsolable. With a dramatic sob, Betty lurched forward and cast off the arms of her supportive friends. She staggered toward the grave with outstretched arms.

Tony had made considerable headway on the hole—but he was still digging in the grave site. As Betty staggered in his direction, Tony paused to lean on his shovel and cast a questioning look at Ernie. Everything seemed to move in slow motion. *This can't be happening,* he thought.

"I miss my bunny!" Betty cried. "I miss my bunny!"

The congregation reacted with shrieks of alarm.

"Poor Betty."

"Somebody grab her!"

Betty teetered on the edge of the hole that Tony had dug for the bunny's grave. Her arms flailed all over the place, like she was losing her balance and about to fall.

Dusty sounded the alarm. "Boss," he shouted. "We got a *diver!*"

"I miss Chester Playboy!" Betty blubbered with a headlong lunge toward the hole.

"She's going for the grave!" Dusty cried.

Ernie grabbed Betty's arm. Dusty grabbed her ankles. They pulled in opposite directions as if it were a Betty tug-of-war.

In the confusion, Ernie automatically blustered through the last thought of his eulogy all over again. "And when the loved ones you love leave you behind!" he shouted.

Swimming Pool's lower lip trembled. Her eyes blinked rapidly, trying to hold back the tears.

"And you don't know where they're going but they're not coming back," Ernie continued.

Swimming Pool's throat got scratchy and dry. She couldn't open her mouth for fear she would blubber.

I'm losing it, she thought. *Here goes. I'm losing it.*

Dusty sat on top of Betty to keep her from falling into the hole. Ernie hooked his shoulder in her armpit and tried to hoist her to her feet.

"And you don't know why and nobody tells you nothing—and your heart is kind of breaking . . ." Ernie shouted.

It was too much for Swimming Pool. She reached her arms out for Betty. Her mouth fell open and her head fell back and she let out the most heartwarming, heart-wrenching, heartfelt wail.

At first it was a wail that felt like it went on for a day. Then it was a wail that went on for a week.

Looking at the wail, you could almost see Swimming Pool's tonsils clanking inside her throat. It was a loud, long, insistent wail. And when it reached the end of its breath, and there was a moment's silence, it was the kind of wail that you expected to start up all over again. Because it was a wail that would go on and on. Many of the mourners later agreed they hadn't heard that kind of wailing since the first week home with their new baby brother.

It was a wail like the first time you touch a hot stove. A wail like the first time you reach for a flower only to get stung by a bee. A wail like the first time somebody takes the training wheels off your bike. Or the first time you get spanked. Or the first time the ice cream lands facedown on the floor. It was a wail like the first time you get blamed and it isn't your fault.

A wail full of trumpets and trombones and tubas. A wail like a parade. Because as it went on, it was the kind of wail that you heard yourself inside and had to join along. And many mourners did. The wailing started with a few and grew and grew—until there were more than a dozen wails inside the one wail.

And when that happened, it became a wail like when you're swinging from a rope and the rope breaks. A wail to make your hair stand on end. A wail to rattle the windows and drive the cats outside. A wail that runs all the way upstairs, slides down the banister, catches its breath, and runs all the way upstairs again.

Even tough old Tony blinked back tears and joined in. Because it had become that kind of wail. A wail that wraps around you and convinces you that you should be wailing too.

Once the wail ended—because at some point, they always do—all the kids were sniffing and catching their breath.

Nobody asked Swimming Pool, but if she'd had to admit it, she would have said that it even felt good to cry.

Every yellow tissue in Betty's box had found its way to some kid's nose—and most of them were strewn across the grass. Betty tossed the empty tissue box aside with a sad little laugh. She grabbed Swimming Pool and hugged her about as close as a stinky aunt does at a family reunion.

"Thanks, Swimming Pool," she enthused. "It's what Chester would have wanted."

Ernie and Dusty leaped into a victorious high-five and cried, "Yes!"

Chapter Thirteen

Talk Salary

After all the kids had cleared the yard, Dusty took on the task of cleaning up. He pulled on a pair of yellow rubber gloves and scooped up all the used tissues. Swimming Pool followed him as he carried a big two-fisted wad of them to the Dumpster.

"Good job, Swimming Pool."

"Thanks," she said, a little bit embarrassed by the huge fuss that everyone was making.

"You're really going to like working here. Ernie is a great boss."

"Yeah, well, we'll see," she said with a doubtful edge. Swimming Pool lifted the Dumpster lid and Dusty dropped the tissues inside. She let the lid drop with a loud *bang.*

Behind the fence, they heard Ernie shouting, "Swimming Pool! Where are you, anyway?"

Swimming Pool jerked a thumb in Ernie's general direction and muttered, "Kind of high maintenance, isn't he?" A second later, Ernie appeared at the gate.

"Oh, there you are," he said enthusiastically. "Good job, Swimming Pool! What did I say? A buck?"

Swimming Pool balked. "Hey! You said a buck fifty!"

"Okay, okay. A buck fifty." Ernie foraged in his pockets for change. "Walk with me, Swimming Pool. I want to talk to you."

Ernie headed down the alley for his house. Swimming Pool tossed a look back at Dusty before she began to follow. Dusty gave her a big thumbs-up and went back into the cemetery to finish the cleanup.

"So, Swimming Pool," Ernie began, "how come I never seen you around here before?"

"I don't know where you been hiding. I been around."

"Just figured I would have been introduced to a girl with your potential."

Swimming Pool was thrown by that remark. "What is that supposed to mean?" she said with a tinge of annoyance.

Ernie backpedaled. "Nothing, nothing." He didn't want to offend the girl who could turn his business around.

They walked in silence for a moment.

Ernie didn't want to talk business in the alley. He wanted to wait until they got to his back stoop. But if he couldn't talk business, Ernie didn't really know what else to talk about.

Swimming Pool opted for small talk. She looked up at the funny old brownstones that lined the alley. "Cool houses," Swimming Pool said, making chitchat about nothing.

"My mom always said they're the Dowagers 'cause they're old and crotchety," Ernie said.

"I don't get it," Swimming Pool said.

"Neither do I." Ernie shrugged.

When they reached Ernie's back stoop, Mister Doggie was whining and scratching inside the screen door. "That your dog?" Swimming Pool asked.

"Yeah. He's not allowed out much," Ernie said with a dismissive wave. "He's too old and too little. But enough about the dog." He turned toward Swimming Pool with purpose. "Listen, Swimming Pool, if you ever want to do this again—"

"Hold it right there." Swimming Pool held out her hand. She could see the job pitch coming. "Talk to me about salary," she said.

"Wha—salary?" Ernie asked.

"Talk salary. I'm all ears. And I'm not greedy. Say fifteen bucks a week."

"Fifteen bucks!" Ernie snapped.

"Hey, I see what kind of business you got. Kids got pets dropping right and left. Do the math! You need someone dependable. Someone on salary."

Ernie hesitated. He knew that Swimming Pool made sense. He wasn't stalling. He was doing the math in his head. "Fifteen bucks? Okay, that sounds . . . deal," he said, and held out his hand.

"Hold up, no deal yet." Swimming Pool flagged his hand away. "I go on salary, and then in six weeks, we talk about a raise."

"A raise?" Ernie snapped again. "You haven't even started working—talking about a raise!"

"Okay, fine," she said. "Find yourself another crybaby." Swimming Pool turned to go.

Ernie raced down the back stoop to block her path. "Wait, Swimming Pool," he cried. He couldn't afford to let Swimming Pool get away. Not after word got around about the great job she had done at that funeral today.

He wiped his hand off on his hip pocket and extended it again. "Hard bargain, kid," he said. "Deal."

"Deal." Swimming Pool shrugged. This had been easier than she thought.

They shook hands.

"Okay, then," Ernie automatically enthused. "Let's synchronize our watches. Time is money!"

"What are you talking about?" Swimming Pool responded.

"I got you on salary, right? So your time belongs to me."

"But—" Swimming Pool tried to interrupt, but Ernie was on a roll. She couldn't get a word in edgewise.

"I got fifteen funerals scheduled for next week. I

need your school schedule, your bus number, your home phone, and your social security number."

"Right," Swimming Pool responded with a crisp and efficient snap.

"And if you got a taste for Saturday-morning cartoons, you can lose it right now."

"Right," said Swimming Pool—but inside, she was thinking, *Oh, man.*

Ernie studied his notebook. "I'm checking tomorrow and I'm looking at one, two—no, three funerals scheduled for tomorrow. Including Matt and that Frisky."

"Any way you can pass me the stats on the deceased before the actual event?" Swimming Pool asked.

"Check with the Dust Man. He keeps all that on file. In fact, stop by Dusty's toolshed first thing in the morning to get briefed on the day's events."

With that, Ernie closed his notebook and headed inside. "Good doing business with you, Swimming Pool."

Swimming Pool was left standing on the step, still setting the time on her wristwatch. As she headed down the stairs toward Dusty's toolshed, she was thinking, *What have I gotten myself into?*

The next morning, Swimming Pool found out.

"Guinea pig," Dusty announced as he handed Swimming Pool a cookie tin festooned with blue ribbons. "And this is the owner, Gina," he continued, pointing toward a timid little girl in the corner of his toolshed.

Swimming Pool jumped. The girl was so quiet that Swimming Pool hadn't even noticed her standing there.

"Technically, *not* a guinea pig," Gina commented in a shy but deliberate voice. "Technically, *Cavia cobaya*. A small, stout-bodied, short-eared, nearly hairless domesticated rodent."

"Whatever," Dusty said. "Named Gus."

"Actually, Gustavus. As in Caesar," Gina offered by way of correction. "Length, twenty-five centimeters; weight, nine hundred and fifty grams."

"Any personality traits? Personal habits? Characteristics?" Swimming Pool asked.

"Known to nibble celery," Dusty read off his report.

"Sometimes a dog biscuit and a little bit of cheese," Gina specified, demonstrating the size with a pinch of her fingers.

"Statistically, the head of the class. Just like his owner, Gina," Dusty said with a nod toward the genius in the corner.

Gina gave a little salute. "The one and only," she replied with a slight quiver in her voice. "Albeit minus Gustavus."

"Cause of death?" Swimming Pool asked.

Gina crumbled into tears. "I hugged him too much!" she said.

Dusty looked awkwardly at Swimming Pool as

Gina continued to cry. Neither one of them knew what to do.

After a moment, Swimming Pool rounded the workbench and carefully wrapped an arm around Gina's shoulders. "There, there," Swimming Pool said. Gina cried even harder after that.

Swimming Pool glanced over Gina's head at Dusty with a look that said, "What have you gotten me into here, Dusty?"

But Dusty smiled back. Swimming Pool was going to work out just fine.

Chapter Fourteen

Not Like Mom

Ernie's business had taken off in a big way. On the one hand, of course, this was a great thing. On the other hand, it was a headache like never before.

"So, like, every night," Ernie was saying, "I get home from school—or like after a funeral that day—and I have to totally switch hats and just pretend I'm just a kid. Like the business isn't going on at all."

It was a confounding dilemma.

Ernie was confiding these thoughts to Dusty in the toolshed. It was something he'd gotten comfortable doing after they knocked off a funeral or two in the afternoon. He'd hang out with Dusty and shoot the breeze while Dusty worked on the boxes for the next day's run of funeral services.

"It's like living a double life," Ernie groused. "I go home for supper and I'm thinking business, but I can't talk business."

Dusty was sprinkling glitter on a gerbil wheel that he'd already sprayed with glue. Although he'd never mentioned it, Dusty had to admit he kind of enjoyed sorting through problems with Ernie. It made him feel connected.

And of course, Dusty knew all about Red's threat to ground Ernie if he was caught working on any more "cockamamie business schemes."

"It seems kind of kooky, though," said Dusty. "I mean, the funeral biz—it's not such a cockamamie thing." Dusty picked up a handful of jelly beans and studied the gerbil wheel. "It's a good thing. Kids like it. Can't you just tell your dad—"

Ernie cut him off. "If Dad finds out I started another business, I'm grounded," he insisted. "No ifs, ands, or buts. And if I'm grounded, who's going to run the business?"

Ernie had a point there. "We couldn't do it without you," said Dusty as he hot-glued the jelly beans to the gerbil wheel.

"My point exactly."

"So if you can't tell your dad about the business," Dusty asked—because it seemed as if business was all Ernie ever talked about with Dusty—"what do you talk about?"

"I don't know." Ernie shrugged. "Math class, baseball scores, geography tests. Nothing. I don't know if I'm going to be able to get used to this. I don't know how much more of this I can take!"

Ernie wasn't referring to the funeral business. He was referring to the big new development in Ernie's household.

Ernie and Red were eating supper at the dinner table.

Red had some new idea that they needed to sit down and eat as a family. Ernie went along with it, because otherwise he wasn't going to get fed. But it wasn't easy.

It had all started the night of the pizza box.

Ernie got home one day after the usual round of funerals down the alley. He charged into his kitchen and let out a loud whistle.

"Hey, Mister Doggie!" he cried. Usually Mister Doggie came running at the sound of the whistle. When he didn't, Ernie knew how to get his attention. He would rattle Mister Doggie's dog bowl, or else he would shake the box of dog biscuits. If neither of those tactics worked, Ernie would jiggle Mister Doggie's favorite dog toy.

That day, for some reason, Mister Doggie wasn't responding. Ernie had tried all his usual tricks and he still wasn't seeing that dog. He even grabbed the windup clock from Mister Doggie's dog bed and gave it a healthy crank.

Ticktock, the clock said—but still no doggie.

Ernie walked into the living room and found

Red sitting in front of the television, just about to open a large box of pizza.

"Grab yourself a plate," Red said over his shoulder. "Your mother would kill me if I didn't make you get a plate."

"Have you seen the canine?" Ernie asked.

"You mean Mister Doggie?" said Red.

"You know I hate that name," Ernie responded.

Red shrugged. "He's getting deaf," he said. "He'll come out when he's hungry. Go grab a plate."

Instead of grabbing a plate, Ernie just reached into the box and grabbed a slab of pizza. His gaze turned to the television—and Red joined him.

Ernie and Red sat together, gnawing on pizza and watching TV. Neither one of them used a plate.

Every now and then, during the pizza, they laughed at the same line in the television show. And every now and then Ernie noticed that Red was looking at him. It was like Red was watching Ernie laugh. But still, neither one of them said a word.

When the pizza was done and the television show was over, Red turned to Ernie and said, "Your turn to do the dishes."

Ernie stood up, crumpled the pizza box, and spanked his hands clean. "Dishes done," he said— and let out a healthy belch.

"Nice," Red said with a disapproving scowl.

"Hey, Dad," Ernie said brightly, like he'd just had a brilliant idea. "Your turn to walk the dog."

Score one for Ernie. He laughed and hooted and capered down the hall as though he had just scored a touchdown and was dancing in the end zone. "Yes! Yes! Yes!" he cried.

But Red was still watching Ernie. He wasn't laughing and it seemed like he had something on his mind.

When Ernie got home the next night, he found Red in the kitchen. His sleeves were rolled and he was singing some silly song that Ernie had never heard before. At the sound of the door closing, Red called out his name.

"Ernie!"

Mister Doggie appeared around the corner and ran down the hall. Ernie gave him a friendly jostle. "Perk up, buddy?" he said. "Feeling better?"

He rounded the corner into the dining room, and the table was covered with Chinese-food containers. That wasn't so strange, in and of itself. But there was Red, dropping place mats and arranging the silverware and paper-wrapped chopsticks into table settings with all the flourish of a fancy chef.

"What are you doing?" Ernie asked.

"I got food," Red said as though nothing was different in the least.

Ernie glanced at the den and stuck his thumb in the direction of the television set. "We can't eat in front of the TV?"

"Not tonight," said Red. "I got this new rule. We sit at the table and eat."

Ernie rumpled his brow. "'Cause why?" he asked.

"'Cause it's called a dining-room table, and we ought to use it for something besides reading the newspaper and tossing the mail. Table's set. Wash up."

"Okay already," Ernie said. He walked into the kitchen—and once he had left the room, he heard Red add one last little explanation, which sounded like the reason for the whole thing in the first place.

"Besides," Red said, "it's a chance for us to sit down and talk. Like family. About time we started acting more like a family around here."

Family. That was the kicker. Ernie reached for the soap. *Family*, he thought as he washed his hands, *that's what this is really about.*

"So from now on," Red announced like he was making a declaration, "every night, at six-thirty sharp, we are having dinner at the dinner table, hands washed—and we are going to have a little talk. Like family."

Ernie groaned—but not so Red could hear.

Sadly, the truth was, once Ernie and Red sat down over the Chinese food, they still couldn't find a whole lot to talk about. They'd talk about the scores in a ball game, and that subject would dry up. They'd talk about school, and that subject would dry up. And then they'd sit there with their chopsticks in silence.

In fact, after a while, the only sound in the dining room was the gentle *click-click* of chopsticks. That is, until the quiet in the room was shattered by the unexpected ringing of Ernie's cell phone.

Ernie almost dropped an egg roll. *I forgot to turn the phone off!* he thought.

At two rings, Red cocked an ear. Even Mister Doggie cocked an ear.

Ernie just munched on his egg roll, feigning nonchalance.

"What's that noise?" Red asked.

"I don't hear anything," Ernie said innocently.

"It's a telephone," Red insisted.

Ernie shrugged as if he hadn't a clue. "Must be the neighbors'. Good wonton, Dad."

After two more rings, the cell phone finally stopped. *Whew*, thought Ernie. *No more ringing.*

Red listened to the silence. "Guess you were right," he said with a shrug. He pushed a container toward Ernie. "There's more Chinese noodles," he said. Ernie helped himself.

Red sat back and wiped his mouth with the paper napkin. "How you doing lately? School okay?" he asked.

"Who wants to know?"

"I do," said Red. "That's why it was me asking."

Ernie decided to cut to the chase. He figured he could take care of family hour with one remark. He looked up from the chow mein and said, "I never see you."

Red sighed. "I'm sorry about that, Ernie," he said. "You know I've been working hard lately. Trying to, you know, do a good job. Make a success."

"All you do is work," Ernie added.

Red flinched. He had been feeling guilty before, but now he was a little peeved. It's not easy to work all day and have the effort go unappreciated at home. "Hey," he snapped. "Work puts food on this table."

"Yeah, but not like it's homemade," Ernie said. He held up half an egg roll and let it drop onto his plate. It landed with a *thunk*.

Red frowned. He propped an elbow on the table and scratched his head. He looked across the table at the empty Chinese-food containers and sighed. Red dropped his chopsticks into the rice bowl. He didn't want his well-intended attempt to start a family routine to turn into another fight with Ernie. "Well, no," he said. "It's not homemade. At least . . . not like your mom made."

When Red said that, Ernie regretted that he'd spoken up in the first place. "Nope," Ernie agreed. "Not like Mom."

It was precisely at that moment that Ernie's cell phone decided to start ringing again. Ernie fidgeted nervously. "May I be excused?" he asked.

Red reluctantly nodded and Ernie left the room. He hustled up the stairs to his room and waited to answer the call until after his bedroom door was closed. As he'd suspected, it was some kid calling to schedule a funeral.

Red sat in the dining room for several minutes before he got up to get the garbage can, dragged it over to the table, and started tossing the empty Chinese-food containers into it.

Chapter Fifteen

Punching the Clock

*S*wimming *Pool was* having a hard time getting rid of the Little League team.

Kip, one of the team captains, approached Swimming Pool during recess. "Hey, Swimming Pool. Big game today," said Kip. "You gonna be able to cover for Danny on third?"

Swimming Pool was drinking from a water fountain, so most of her response came back during a slurp. "Can't today, Kip," she said. "Ernie's got two funerals scheduled for this afternoon."

"But Swimming Pool," Kip pleaded, "it's the series final. We face off against the Army Girls."

"Crying shame, Kip," Swimming Pool replied. "But I got work to do."

"But you're our secret weapon," Kip argued.

"No can do," said Swimming Pool.

"But—but—but—but . . . ," Kip stammered.

"Can't you talk to Ernie? Can't you get the time off?"

It's not like Swimming Pool hadn't tried. She had asked Ernie before, but all she got was trouble.

"I don't want to hear about a ball game," Ernie had barked. "I got you on salary. Time is money. I'm looking at my watch and it says you work for me."

"No can do," Swimming Pool sighed to Kip with a sad shrug. "I'm punching the clock."

"But what am I gonna tell the team?" Kip begged.

"Tell 'em I got a funeral," said Swimming Pool.

When Swimming Pool got home that afternoon, she ran upstairs to get the purple dress. On the way, she stopped by the door to Rick's old room. Sometimes Swimming Pool would go in there and just sit at the drum set Rick had left behind. She didn't dare take a stab at playing the drums, for fear her other brothers would tease her about it. But sometimes it was enough to sit in the chair and run her finger against the edge of the cymbal.

But Swimming Pool didn't have time to sit at the drum set today. Ernie was expecting her at the cemetery. And besides, she didn't feel like getting maudlin before work.

She grabbed the purple dress and stuffed it into her knapsack. Then she charged downstairs to grab a quick snack in the kitchen before heading over to the cemetery.

She jerked open the refrigerator and looked inside—the shelves were surprisingly empty. Unless she was in the mood for eggs. Or celery.

That was odd.

Swimming Pool checked the bread box and the cookie jar too—but they were empty. The pantry was basically empty too. Swimming Pool couldn't figure it out.

Something very odd was going on.

Just then she heard a noise from the garage. She opened the door to check it out, and that's when she saw her long-lost brother.

Sure enough. It was Rick. He was crouching over a laundry basket, stuffing clean towels next to a bunch of food supplies.

"Not you again," Swimming Pool grunted with fake annoyance.

Rick jumped, totally startled. She had gotten him good. "Snorkelpuss. You scared me."

"What are you doing here?" she asked.

Rick shrugged. "Sneaked in with the key under the rock. Grabbing a few more things."

"Yeah. Like the peanut butter." Swimming Pool pointed to the jar stashed in the laundry basket.

"I don't need it, I just figured—"

"Forget about it, Rick. Take the peanut butter."

"I don't need it," Rick insisted. "It's just that I've been a little low on cash flow lately."

Swimming Pool took a moment to look at Rick.

She had figured that cash flow was part of the problem.

"Hey," she said, trying to make this as casual as possible. "I got something for you."

She climbed onto the washer and reached into the cupboard for her secret coffee can. She pulled off the lid and took out a small roll of cash. "Ta-da!" she cried, twirling the cash under Rick's nose.

"Where'd you get the cash?" he asked.

"I been working."

"Working at what?"

"I got this job. No big deal. I live at home. My life is cheap. I got you this money."

"I'm not taking your money, Pool."

"Take it," she insisted. "I got it for you."

"Nah, I got my pride, you know." Rick backed off.

"Yeah. Your pride and our peanut butter," Swimming Pool argued.

Rick looked at Swimming Pool as though she'd just hit him below the belt.

"Ouch," he said.

Swimming Pool shrugged. "Hey, I didn't mean anything by it," she said. But Rick had already scooped up his laundry basket and was hustling down the driveway.

"I'm outta here," Rick called back over his shoulder. "Don't tell Dad you saw me."

"As if I would," Swimming Pool answered, raising her arm to wave good-bye.

Rick didn't even turn back to notice her wave.

Swimming Pool dropped her arm and mouthed the word "Polo."

She was determined to get the money she'd saved to Rick. Otherwise, there was no point to working so hard.

But how?

Chapter Sixteen

Dead Iguana

The Dead Iguana Funeral was Ernie's biggest hit yet.

Jeremy was the name of the kid who owned the dead iguana. And truthfully, Jeremy wasn't the most popular kid around. He was short and kind of chubby. He wore thick glasses and kept to himself most of the time. Most of the kids at school couldn't even remember Jeremy's name. He was pretty much known as the Kid with the Glasses.

"I don't really have any friends," Jeremy admitted to Ernie. "But I don't mind. I have my iguana."

"You mean 'had,'" Ernie corrected him.

Swimming Pool threw an elbow at Ernie. She glared at him briefly with a look that said, "You can be so insensitive at times." She stepped around him to drape an arm around Jeremy. "Did your iguana have a name?" she asked gently.

"No, not really." Jeremy shrugged. "I just called him Iguana."

Swimming Pool nodded, and she really didn't know what to ask next. Usually kids opened right up when you asked them about their pet. But getting Jeremy to open up was like working on a can of tuna with a broken pencil. "Did you have Iguana long?" is what she eventually asked.

"Oh, yeah. Since he was a baby. Since he was about this long," Jeremy said, and measured out about five inches with his fingers.

"How big is he now?"

"About two feet," Jeremy replied. "Tip to tail. Except, of course, he's dead."

"That's it!" Ernie snapped. He had been getting a little impatient with Swimming Pool's counseling session.

"Listen," he said, squaring off against Jeremy, "we could do a private burial, just you and your iguana, but that isn't what we do best. I mean, it's kind of a waste of our time. But if we do an open-box burial—and give all the kids a chance to see your dead iguana . . ."

Jeremy's eyes already looked big behind his glasses. But in that moment, Jeremy's eyes seemed to grow just a little bit wider.

After Ernie talked Jeremy into hosting an open-box iguana funeral, and after word got around about the public viewing of the dead iguana—well,

Jeremy's popularity stock shot up quite a bit. In fact, for the next few days or so, Jeremy was everyone's new best friend.

And when the Saturday arrived for Jeremy's Dead Iguana Funeral, the line of kids at the cemetery stretched across the yard, out the gate, and halfway down the alley. For that Saturday, at least, Jeremy was the most popular kid around.

And Ernie threw a particularly good event. Dusty really outdid himself on the iguana box.

It was an old picnic basket—but Dusty had painted a different shade of green on each loop in the straw weave. The basket was coated with a glossy shellac—two or three layers, so it gave off a really slick shine. In fact, the whole thing looked like it was made of scales, which was Dusty's intention.

Inside, Dusty laid a nest of purple grass left over from Easter. And on top of that was the dead iguana.

Swimming Pool stood at the head of the line, next to the basket, with an arm around Jeremy. She was sobbing appropriately—even though Jeremy just sort of stood there and smiled.

When Swimming Pool reached over and flipped open the lid on the Dead Iguana Box for the public viewing, a gasp went up from the first few mourners. And after that, a buzz of excitement rippled through the kids waiting in line. All the way across the yard, through the gate, and halfway down the block.

Ernie had given Swimming Pool strict instructions to keep the line moving. People could look for five seconds at the dead iguana before Swimming Pool would gently say, "Thank you, move along."

Positioned as she was near the dead iguana, Swimming Pool was able to witness some pretty bad behavior from the mourners, as sometimes happened at events such as these.

Gina, the timid brainiac, whimpered in fear as she approached the iguana box, pretending she was too shy, but then she just had to look. Once she did get a look at the iguana, Swimming Pool could barely pry Gina's fingers away from the box to get her to move along. Gina even tried to snap a photograph.

Betty, the girl with the dead bunny, tossed a withering been-there-done-that look at the dead iguana.

Betty was followed by one of the wisecracking boys from the Little League team, who actually tried to stick his leftover gum inside the box.

"Hey!" Swimming Pool barked. "Save it for the sandlot, mister."

Swimming Pool was surprised to see Tony waiting in line to see the dead iguana. He stepped up to the box and teetered on tiptoe to peer inside with gross-me-out relish.

But the strangest response that Swimming Pool witnessed came from two rather spooky little girls known to have an extensive collection of bugs and lizards and oddball pets.

Their names were Finny and Fanny, and they

were identical twins in matching gray jumpers and matching white blouses. They even wore matching hair braids at the exact same length, at the exact same angle, with the exact same number of colored beads woven into them.

As Swimming Pool later described it to Dusty, when Finny and Fanny reached the Dead Iguana Box, all they did was giggle.

"Giggle?" Dusty asked.

"Giggle," Swimming Pool replied. "I don't know how to describe how creepy it was, Dusty. But you can just imagine. They *giggled*."

And when Finny and Fanny walked away from the iguana box, all Swimming Pool could do was shudder.

Chapter Seventeen

Finny and Fanny

At the tail end of the Dead Iguana Funeral, Ernie was standing in the alley, counting heads for a total attendance record on the crowd and policing kids from cutting into line.

Before the visitation had ended, Finny and Fanny shoved past Ernie to exit the gate and ran together pell-mell down the alley. Only a few minutes later, Finny and Fanny came running back up the alley—only this time they were carrying a brown paper lunch bag.

"Oh, Ernie," said Finny. "We're terribly upset."

"Our hermit crab, Spike," said Fanny, "is terribly, terribly—"

"*Dead*," said Finny. And then the two girls giggled.

"Well, you've come to the right place," Ernie

assured them with a somewhat wary reservation.

"He really liked Elvis," said Finny.

"And he really liked flies," said Fanny.

"Okay, okay," Ernie said. "But it's gonna cost—"

"Oh, we got the money," Finny assured him, sounding perhaps a little too eager. They left the bag with Ernie and scampered down the alley.

Ernie shuddered. He held the bag in his outstretched arm and crossed the alley to Dusty's toolshed. When he opened the door, Dusty and Swimming Pool were having one of their private powwows. Actually, they'd been comparing notes on those creepy twins, Finny and Fanny.

Ernie gave the bag holding Spike a quick toss toward Dusty.

"Here you go, Dusty!" he cried. "Think fast."

Dusty caught the bag and felt the lump inside. "Let me guess," he said with a glance at Swimming Pool. "Finny and Fanny."

Dusty and Swimming Pool exchanged a look. "The Macabre Kids," they said together with a shudder.

"You got it," Ernie answered.

Dusty tossed the bag toward Swimming Pool. "Peuw and euw," she said when the late hermit crab landed in her pitcher's glove.

A couple nights later Ernie had suffered through another difficult dinner with his dad. This time, the ordeal had taken place over spaghetti. Homemade spaghetti.

"I followed the directions," Red had insisted as Ernie held a forkful aloft.

"It still tastes like paste," Ernie said.

After dinner, Red was flipping through the employment section of the newspaper in the den and tossing heavy sighs. Ernie was, to all appearances, doing his math homework at the dining-room table.

"It's not that I mind the work," Red was saying, "it's just that I'm always either late for work . . . or exhausted—"

Ernie interrupted, "Dad? What's seventy percent of ten times eighteen?"

Red raised his eyebrows and shrugged. "Figure it out," he answered.

"Ugh," went Ernie. He hunkered down over his pencil and applied himself to the task. "Ten times eighteen is one hundred and eighty," he muttered. "Divided by ten. Multiplied by seven."

When he had finally done the math, Ernie couldn't help but yelp a victorious "Yes!"

Red looked up from his newspaper.

Ernie flipped open his notebook and entered the sum in his accounts. He'd been balancing books on the business. And the good news was that it was all profit.

"Since when did you start liking math?" Red asked.

Just then the doorbell rang. Red and Ernie looked at each other. "You expecting company?" Red asked.

Ernie shrugged.

Red got up from the sofa to answer the door.

On the front porch stood two rather spooky-looking little girls holding a coffee can. "We're looking for Ernie," the girls announced.

"Ernie! You got company!" Red shouted, and returned to the sofa.

Ernie left the dining room and walked to the door. When he saw that it was Finny and Fanny, he kept his voice low.

"What now, ladies?" he asked.

Ernie took the coffee can from them and tried to keep the conversation as brief as possible. They had their brief exchange and Ernie closed the door, holding the coffee can behind his back to keep it a secret from his dad.

Even so, as he passed through the den on his way back to the dining-room table, Red looked up from his newspaper again. "Glad to see you making friends," he said. "Especially with the ladies."

"Dad!" Ernie cried out.

The next afternoon, Ernie opened the door to the toolshed to find Swimming Pool in yet another powwow with Dusty. He chucked the coffee can at Dusty. "Dead beetle in a coffee can, Dusty," he said. "Work your magic."

Dusty took one look at the coffee can and said, "Let me guess."

Ernie, Dusty, and Swimming Pool chimed in on a chorus of "Finny and Fanny. The Macabre Kids."

"Finny and Fanny want a funeral for a dead beetle?" Dusty asked.

"No questions, Dusty," Ernie admonished.

Swimming Pool and Dusty chimed in on the end of that sentence, "The customer is always right."

With that kind of encouragement, it should have been no surprise when Finny and Fanny accosted Ernie the next day with a cottage cheese container. "Ernie . . . ," they called in unison.

"Hi, Finny. Hi, Fanny," he replied, but without a lot of enthusiasm.

"It's our spider," said Fanny, raising the cottage cheese container up high.

"Ick?" Ernie asked.

"Ick." Finny nodded.

"I didn't know Ick was sick."

"Not sick," Fanny corrected. "Dead. Terribly, terribly—"

"Ick," said Ernie. "No details."

That afternoon, Ernie trotted the cottage cheese container over to Dusty's toolshed. Sure enough, Swimming Pool and Dusty were having another powwow. Ernie was kind of happy that Swimming Pool and Dusty were getting along so well. It meant for a stronger team. But they sure did seem to spend a lot of time whispering about something.

"Brace yourself, Dusty," Ernie said, holding the container aloft. "Ick the Spider."

"Ick," said Dusty, peering inside the container.

"I remember him," said Swimming Pool, peeking over Dusty's shoulder.

Dusty and Swimming Pool exchanged a shudder. "Ick," they said in unison.

"Something simple and dignified," said Ernie. With that, he closed the toolshed door and let Dusty and Swimming Pool get back to whatever they had been talking about.

Of course, only a few days passed by—and Finny and Fanny were accosting Ernie again. They knocked on the door of the toolshed while Ernie, Swimming Pool, and Dusty were having a meeting.

Ernie opened the door and barely suppressed a groan at the sight of Finny and Fanny. "The customer is always right," Ernie reminded himself— even as he thought, *But this Finny/Fanny routine is getting kind of old.*

This time, Finny and Fanny had a tin can.

"Oh, Ernie. We're terribly, terribly—"

"What now?" Ernie asked with a cringe.

"*Woodrow Worm,*" they announced.

Ernie, Dusty, and Swimming Pool issued a collective shudder.

"Worm?" said Dusty. "Sorry, Macabre Kids. No can do."

"We don't do worms," added Swimming Pool.

"Company policy," Ernie declared.

"Bury worms," reiterated Dusty.

"What's the point?" concluded Swimming Pool.

Finny and Fanny issued a joint "harrumph" and stalked off in a huff.

Ernie, Dusty, and Swimming Pool threw high fives and danced a little end-zone jig.

Chapter Eighteen

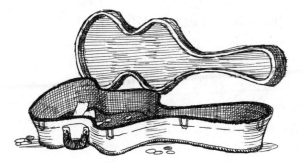

Something Pretty

$\mathcal{S}$wimming Pool arrived at Ernie's place to find Ernie proudly polishing a brand-new bike.

"Hey, Ernie, what's that? A new bike?"

Ernie popped the rag against the shiny fender. "Kids don't wanna see me on an old bike. Creates the wrong impression."

He arched an eyebrow at Swimming Pool and added, "Must be payday, huh?"

"Why do you say that?"

"You're not always so bright and early. Follow me inside."

Ernie dropped the rag and headed up the steps. Pool followed.

When they got inside the kitchen, they were greeted by a clatter of claws as Mister Doggie skittered into the room. Swimming Pool reached down to pat his head. "Hey there, buddy. Sweet puppy."

"He's not a puppy. He's full grown. Actually, he's old for a dog. He's just really small."

"What's his name?"

"Mister Doggie. Stupid name." Ernie gave Mister Doggie's dish a little kick.

Swimming Pool shrugged. "I've heard worse."

"My mom named him," Ernie explained.

Ernie never talked about his mom—and Swimming Pool had been wondering why she had never seen her around the house. It seemed like there were two things that Ernie never talked about: (1) how much money he made, and (2) his mom.

So Swimming Pool asked.

"What happened to your mom, anyway? They get divorced?"

"No. She . . . ," Ernie hesitated. "She got cancer and died."

"Oh. Sorry. How dumb do I feel?"

"I was planning to tell you. Just didn't get around to it yet."

Wow, Swimming Pool thought. "So this whole funeral thing must really be . . . ," she ventured with a gentle wave of her hand.

Ernie jerked his head abruptly. "What?" he said in a flat and defensive voice.

Ouch. Obviously Ernie didn't want to talk about his mother. Swimming Pool dropped it. She turned her attention to Mister Doggie as he curled in his bed next to a windup clock.

"What's with the clock?" she asked.

"My mom put it there. Mister Doggie used to cry in his sleep when he was a puppy. But he thinks the *ticktock, ticktock* is his mom's heart."

This was too embarrassing. Ernie opened a cigar box and peeled out Pool's pay.

"Here, thirteen, fourteen, fifteen dollars." He pressed the bills into Swimming Pool's palm and switched the subject with a certain vigor. "So," he declared. "What you doing with all that money, Pool?"

"Nothing much," she said. Swimming Pool didn't really want to talk about what she did with her money. "Everybody has subjects they don't like to talk about."

As if to rescue her from having to give a better answer, Dusty appeared at the screen door. Both Ernie and Swimming Pool jumped because—for a moment there—Dusty's face through the screen really looked like a monster.

"Boo!" said Dusty. "Hey, Boss. Hey, Pool."

Swimming Pool reached for the screen door to join Dusty outside. "Me and Dusty are headed to the mall," she explained.

"Is that right?" said Ernie. "Off to the mall, eh? Have a good time. Buy yourself something pretty!"

Swimming Pool let the screen door slam as she joined Dusty on the stoop.

"Can you believe how he talks to me?" she said.

• • •

When they got to the mall, Swimming Pool and Dusty were crouched behind a car in the parking lot outside. Dusty was looking through a pair of binoculars. Swimming Pool rested a hand on the binoculars until they were focused on somebody sitting on the sidewalk outside the mall.

"See him?" she asked. "He's sitting with a guitar."

Sure enough, there was her long-lost brother Rick. Dusty took in the sight of the guy playing his guitar on the sidewalk next to his open guitar case.

"What's he doing?" Dusty asked, like he couldn't believe his eyes. "Singing?"

"You got the sound off," Swimming Pool said defensively. "He sings good. Get an eyeful?"

"Think so."

"Okay." She took the binoculars and reached into her pocket. She had a small object wrapped tightly in rubber bands. She pressed it into Dusty's palm and said, "You know what to do."

Swimming Pool and Dusty slipped across the parking lot until they reached the sidewalk where a rather intense Girl Scout was selling cookies behind a card table.

"Meet me back by the cookies," Swimming Pool instructed. Dusty nodded and continued down the sidewalk.

He clutched the object in his fist—so tightly his knuckles were turning white. His heart was racing and it felt like he was holding his breath. Dusty had a lot of performance anxiety when it came to errands like this.

He angled near Rick's guitar case and dropped the object so that it landed right in the center of the felt-covered box. Never breaking his pace, Dusty continued nimbly on his way, trying to look as nonchalant as possible.

Even so, Dusty's whole pass by the guitar case was such a curiously clumsy and contrived thing that Rick paused from his singing and turned to eye the object Dusty had dropped.

Behind the Girl Scout table Swimming Pool lifted her binoculars. She had to refocus to zoom in close on Rick's face. She saw his eyes widen as he considered the object in his hand.

It was a wad of bills.

One-dollar bills, five-dollar bills, and ten-dollar bills, rolled into a tight bundle and fastened with a rubber band.

"Happy Birthday, Rick," she said to herself. Even though it wasn't Rick's birthday at all.

Swimming Pool lowered the binoculars to find Dusty waiting on the other side of the Girl Scout table. He held a box of cookies under each arm and was grinning a triumphant smile.

"Mission accomplished," Dusty said.

Swimming Pool slung an arm around Dusty's shoulders and they started the long walk home.

Chapter Nineteen

We Meet Again

Ernie was taking his new bike for a test-spin around the block. And he was feeling pretty good about life.

When you buy something with your own money, it just feels different somehow. That's what Ernie was thinking as he rode down the street with a new sense of status.

Up ahead Cat Lady was unloading groceries from her car at the curb. But Ernie didn't see Cat Lady. He also didn't see that the grocery bag in Cat Lady's arms was just about to burst. Ernie didn't see the bag burst, but he did see the cans of cat food as they skittered across his path, abruptly turning the street into a treacherous obstacle course.

Ernie skidded right and left and fishtailed a few times on his new bike before screeching to a halt.

He looked up to find Cat Lady holding a shredded paper bag.

"So. Cat Lady. We meet again," he said with a rueful smile.

"I am so sorry!" Cat Lady apologized. She looked at the cat food all over the street and said, "How dreadful."

Ernie picked up one can and flipped it over in his hand. "So," he said, "I guess it is true."

"What is true?"

Ernie tossed the can into the air and caught it again. "That you fatten up your cats and eat Fat-Cat Stew," he said with a smile.

Cat Lady insisted that it wasn't necessary, but Ernie felt obliged to help her track down her cat food and carry the cans into the house. And so it was that Ernie found himself carting an armful of cat food cans into Cat Lady's clean and comfortable kitchen.

Cat Lady stacked the cans on the counter. "Fat-Cat Stew," she announced like she was reciting a recipe. "Oregano, paprika, salt to taste, garnish with parsley and serve."

"You're kidding, right?" Ernie asked, spilling the cans in his arms onto the countertop.

Cat Lady had one of those senses of humor where you couldn't tell whether she was kidding or not.

"Watch," Cat Lady instructed. "Feeding time!" she cried as she placed a can of cat food on the counter and opened a drawer to find a can opener.

At the very sound of the drawer, much less the rattle of the can opener, cats came running from every corner of the house.

Two cats bounced off the back of a chair, and another cat raced under the dining-room table. One cat sprang frantically from the windowsill to a stool and to the floor, and then came to curl languidly around Cat Lady's ankles as though he'd just done nothing at all.

Ernie had to be careful where he stepped to stay out of the way of all the cats. He pressed back against the refrigerator. That's when Ernie happened to notice his flyer stuck to the refrigerator with a magnet. The one that Dusty had illustrated in art class with the drawing of the puppy with wings.

Ernie plucked the flyer out from behind the magnet. "Ahem," he announced as he waved the flyer in the air. "Miss me much?"

"Okay, Ernie," said Cat Lady. "I'm busted. What's up with those funerals? Are you for real?"

"Yes, ma'am," Ernie insisted. "We've got a beautiful private cemetery—conveniently located just across the alley, halfway down the block."

"You mean that old abandoned lot?"

"That's the one." Ernie smiled and barked, "Hey!" as a cat leaped into his arms.

Another cat crawled from the counter into Cat Lady's hands. It was the cat numbered sixty-two that Ernie had met before. Cat #62 was an older cat, and it looked like he had packed on a few pounds.

Cat Lady cradled Cat #62 against her shoulder and scratched behind his ears. He mewed repeatedly, as though he was trying to say something but knew only one word.

Cat Lady answered as if she understood Cat #62 completely. "I know, I know," she said soothingly. "The younger cats never leave any food for you."

"They're very dear," she said to Ernie, looking right into the cat's face. "But not getting any younger," she added, tossing a glance at Ernie. "And a few of them have arched into that ominous ninth lifetime."

"It's true that cats have nine lives?" Ernie asked.

"It's true around this house," Cat Lady replied.

Ernie figured this was a good time to launch into his spiel. "Well, just so you know, we offer visitation, burial, optional wake, eulogy, internment—and the crier. All inclusive at one low price."

"The crier?" Cat Lady asked. "What is the crier?"

"You're the one who suggested it," Ernie said. "You said a funeral should be all boo-hoo-hoo. Sobbing and crying and blubbering. So we got this girl who cries. She's real professional."

Cat Lady grinned and let out a haughty guffaw. "Professional tears," she said as she laughed. "That's brilliant. . . . And how much do you charge?"

Ernie scrunched his face like he was doing the

math and trying to cut Cat Lady a special deal. "Um, *fifteen* dollars. It's usually twenty, but you got so many cats, I could reintroduce that bulk rate."

During the negotiation, Cat Lady rinsed off a clump of fresh grapes she'd taken from a grocery bag and extended some to share with Ernie.

"Fifteen bucks, eh?" she said. "That's a lot of money."

"But we're a full-service operation," Ernie explained. "We'd pick up the cat, give it a specially designed box, its own private lot, and a full-scale burial. All included in one low price."

"Well, let's see," Cat Lady mused. "It still depends. Who've you got there? Who's buried in your cemetery?"

Ernie sighed and rolled his eyes. "It's getting kind of crowded," he admitted. "Let's see. We got Jo-Jo's ferret, Benny's hamster, Charlotte's para-keet, Betty's bunny—"

Cat Lady interrupted him. "Betty's bunny? Chester? You have Chester Playboy?"

"You knew Chester?" said Ernie.

Cat Lady shook her head like it was such a cry-ing shame.

"Oh, Chester Playboy," she said. "I loved that bunny."

When Ernie caught up with Swimming Pool and Dusty back in Dusty's toolshed, he could hardly contain his enthusiasm.

"A bazillion cats!" he yelped as he chomped down on a cookie from the Girl Scout boxes spread open on the table.

"Bazillion's not a number," Dusty corrected him.

"So a quadrillion!" Ernie insisted. "You do the math. We're set for life! Business is booming! Life is sweet! Gimme another cookie."

Even Swimming Pool had to agree that business was good and life was sweet. She leaned back to contemplate her cookie. "I bite mine around the edges," she announced.

Dusty held a cookie up and said, "I let mine dissolve under my tongue." With that, he opened his mouth and dropped the cookie inside, snapping his mouth shut like a cat with a canary. Swimming Pool laughed.

Ernie pulled another cookie from the box. "I drop mine in my milk and let it get soggy," he declared with relish. "Then I slide it into my mouth."

"Euw!" Swimming Pool and Dusty cried. And they all laughed.

Since the talk had turned to cookies, instead of the business, it was a safe bet that this company had turned into a circle of friends.

Chapter Twenty

Out of Control

𝒟*usty was out* of control.

Everyone agreed that Dusty did a beautiful job. Each funeral box was a sight to behold, and each funeral he staged was more spectacular than the last. Customers were full of the highest praise for the work that Dusty did.

But Swimming Pool and Ernie were secretly beginning to wonder just where it would all end.

Kip's terrier, Kirby, had put in three admirable years with the Little League team. So when Kirby passed on, his funeral was an extremely well-attended event.

The entire Little League team was lined up—in uniform—with their caps over their heart in fond memory of Kirby. Swimming Pool ceremoniously circled the grave site to present Kip with Kirby's empty dog leash.

At a nod from Swimming Pool a solemn group of kids played "Taps" on their kazoos. While the congregation listened, a thin roar built overhead and grew louder and louder.

When the congregation finally looked up, they saw four radio-controlled airplanes flying overhead in strategic formation. Tony was manning the controls from behind one of the trees.

That was impressive enough. But at another nod from Swimming Pool, Dusty scrambled to set off a twenty-one-bottle-rocket salute that fizzled across the sky.

Well.

Kip crumbled onto Swimming Pool's shoulder. And even the toughest kid on the Little League team had to bite his lip to hold back the tears.

Everyone agreed that Dusty had done a beautiful job.

But when it was all over and they were picking up the leftover bottle rockets from the grass, Swimming Pool found a moment to mutter to Ernie, "Aren't these things getting a little . . . out of control?"

Ernie replied, "You must be reading my mind."

But it didn't stop there.

When Kiwi's canary finally died, Ernie said, "Great!" because he knew that Dusty had already finished the bird's box. It was that Crystal Capsule for Kiwi's Canary he'd seen on Dusty's workbench. He stopped by Dusty's toolshed to break the news about Kiwi's canary and track down the box.

"Oh, no, Boss," Dusty protested, "we can't pass off Kiwi with one lousy milk carton. We've gotten too big for that."

"Too big for what?" Ernie asked.

Instead of answering, Dusty pulled a roll of sketches out of his suitcase and spread them across the workbench.

Ernie looked at the drawings, but one thing wasn't clear. The drawing showed a group of kids moving down the alley. "What am I looking at?" he asked.

"It's a parade, Boss," said Dusty.

"I still don't understand," said Ernie. He was kind of hoping the whole idea would just go away.

"In New Orleans, people hold funerals with a jazz march through the streets. And since Kiwi's canary was a songbird, I thought we ought to do something kind of musical," Dusty explained.

Ernie smacked his head with the palm of his hand. "Can't things just stay small?" he asked. "Why do we have to do these big productions all the time?"

"You're the one who wanted the business to grow, Boss," Dusty replied.

"I meant the profits," said Ernie, "not the expenses." He rolled up the drawings and handed them back to Dusty.

"But Kiwi thinks it's a great idea," Dusty protested.

"You already showed these drawings to Kiwi?" Ernie asked.

"Yeah, and I think she's down on the books for Saturday," Dusty answered.

Ernie smacked his head again.

And so it was that Swimming Pool draped her arm around Kiwi on Saturday morning as they led a large crowd of kids in a slow-moving procession down the alley. Dusty had recruited band kids to play "Saint James Infirmary" on the tuba, the clarinet, an accordion, and a bass drum.

Kiwi carried the Crystal Capsule for Kiwi's Canary. And other kids carried colorful umbrellas or tall poles festooned with ribbons and fanciful bird-cages—another Dusty creation.

"Be strong, Kiwi," Swimming Pool counseled. "Superfly would have wanted it that way."

"Oh, Swimming Pool," Kiwi sniffled, and sighed. "You've been so wonderful about everything."

"Courage, Kiwi, courage," she urged.

When they arrived at the cemetery, Kiwi turned to join the mourners in a cluster about the grave site as Tony placed Superfly into his final resting place.

Swimming Pool lagged behind and waited for Ernie, who was drawing up the end of the parade, counting heads and adding up a wad of bills. Together, they watched as the parade trailed through the gate and into the cemetery.

"Quite a hullabaloo," Swimming Pool sighed.

"Too true, too true," Ernie agreed.

A look passed between them that said things were definitely getting out of control.

"Makes you kind of wonder where it's all going to end," Swimming Pool ventured.

Ernie raised his shoulders up to his ears. "That's the million-dollar question," he said.

At that moment, Dusty stepped through the gate and joined them in the alley. He was glowing with pride about how well the parade had gone.

"Good job, Dusty!" Swimming Pool enthused.

"Always count on the Dust Man," Ernie agreed, scruffing the hair on Dusty's head.

"Hey, Boss," Dusty said. "Have I ever said thank you? I love my job. Just love it. Not every kid can say 'I love what I do.'"

Dusty ran back inside to continue supervising the burial.

Swimming Pool could tell that Ernie was really touched by Dusty's admission. Even so, she asked again, "Where's it all going to end, Ernie?"

Ernie shook his head. "With loyalty like that," he said, "who can say?"

Chapter Twenty-one

An Unexpected Eden

€arly one evening, Red took Mister Doggie for a walk down the alley. Mister Doggie was moving slower than usual these days, so Red thought it might be a good idea if he took his sweet time.

As he strolled slowly down the alley, Red checked out the gingerbread on the Dowagers, just like he and his wife used to in the days when they had first moved to this neighborhood. Back when they were walking Mister Doggie—and pushing Ernie in a stroller.

When Red got halfway down the alley, he noticed a long green hose running from a toolshed behind one of the brownstones, across the alley, and into an old abandoned lot.

He glanced at the No Trespassing sign on the

ground beside the broken-up gate—and pushed curiously through into the lot.

Red tracked the hose until he reached a vacillating sprinkler head that sent a gentle spray across what actually turned out to be a lovely little garden. In fact, Red was surprised to find that he was standing in an unexpected Eden.

Red was even more surprised to realize that a young woman was standing at the far end of the garden. She held what appeared to be a bouquet of handpicked flowers.

Red did not recognize the woman, but Ernie would have recognized her. It was Cat Lady—only she had combed her hair and put on a pretty dress. Cat Lady had pulled her act together.

"Excuse me?" she called out to Red.

"I'm sorry . . . yes?" Red replied.

In twisting back to speak to the young woman, Red stumbled over the sprinkler head and narrowly avoided spritzing Cat Lady with the water. He staggered awkwardly over the hose and was not successful in staying on his feet. They flew out from underneath him and he ended up suffering a tumble in the wet grass. Red was down for the count with damp trousers.

Mister Doggie charged to Red's side, barking at him to get up.

"I'm okay. I'm okay!" Red called out.

"Oh, no!" Cat Lady protested. "Your trousers are all—"

"It's all right. Really."

"I feel completely responsible," Cat Lady urged.

"No. Really," Red insisted. "How can I help you?"

Cat Lady hedged, and gestured awkwardly about the yard in the failing light. "I'm looking for . . . Chester Playboy," she said.

"Chester Playboy?" Red asked, positively flummoxed.

Cat Lady was embarrassed that she had even asked. "Not to worry," she said. "I'll just leave these here for everyone to enjoy." She placed the flowers on the bench underneath the trestle. And with a smile and a nod, she stepped out of the garden.

Red watched curiously as Cat Lady stepped through the grass.

He walked farther on and glanced down. There was something lying on the lawn. Looking closer, he found a cupcake with a candle, some Goldfish crackers, and a cat toy.

What the . . . ? thought Red.

Chapter Twenty-two

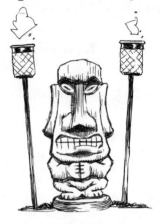

A Raise, a Raise, a Raise

𝒯*he funeral schedule* was getting tighter and tighter. On the worst days, they often had three or four funerals back-to-back. Saturdays were especially stressful. On the particular Saturday in question, the schedule began with a funeral for a gerbil named Scarlett. The event had a *Gone with the Wind* theme.

Swimming Pool and Dusty waved a sad farewell to the departing mourners—several little girls in hoopskirts with parasols. "Good job, Swimming Pool," Ernie said through clenched teeth.

"Another one bites the dust," muttered Dusty.

Once the girls were gone, Swimming Pool turned back toward Ernie. "These four-show days are murder," she griped.

"Tell me about it," said Ernie. They exchanged

low fives all around, like a seasoned ball team after a particularly good game. Then they took a moment to catch their breath and launched into the next event.

"What's on the schedule?" Swimming Pool called. Dusty was already tugging wisteria and Spanish moss off the tree branches. Tony was hurriedly leading a dog-drawn caisson off the yard. "Who's next? What's next?" Swimming Pool cried.

Ernie checked his clipboard. "Island Luau for Polynesian Pete!" he read.

"That's Finny and Fanny's turtle," Dusty added.

Under his breath, Ernie muttered, "Shouldn't have let that turtle play in the driveway in the first place." Then he shouted, "Faster, faster, faster! Dusty! We're gonna need the torches, the volcano, and the tiki god!"

Dusty and Tony toted a long, white Corinthian column across the lawn. That was the last trace of the *Gone with the Wind* theme. "I'm on it, Boss," Dusty shouted back—almost tripping in a hole, sending the column swinging overhead. Both Swimming Pool and Ernie ducked so the column wouldn't whack them in the head.

Even though the job was demanding, Ernie always kept his cool during times like these. He seemed to revel in the chaos. "If we're busy, we got business," is what Ernie would say.

Swimming Pool grabbed Ernie's elbow and pulled him aside. "Ernie," she said, "can we call it payday now so I can get out of here after?"

"Absolutamente," Ernie answered. "Buy yourself something pretty." He reached into his pocket for a wad of cash and started peeling off bills. "A week's pay," Ernie declared. He pulled out a ten and some singles. "Ten and . . . thirteen, fourteen, fifteen bucks," he counted as he pressed the bills into Swimming Pool's palm.

Swimming Pool looked down at the bills in her hand. She clenched her teeth. Ernie had promised a raise in six weeks—but over the course of the six weeks that had now come and gone, Swimming Pool had learned enough about Ernie to expect a battle on this point.

"Not fifteen," she said emphatically.

"What are you talking about? That's fifteen bucks."

"Whoa, wait a minute, Ernie. Not fifteen bucks! It's been more than six weeks since I started. I'm due for a raise."

Ernie hemmed and hawed as though Swimming Pool had caught him at a bad moment. "Oh, yeah, I been meaning to talk to you about that . . ."

"*Raise*," Swimming Pool emphasized. "Talk about the *raise*."

Dusty was dragging in the tiki god, a massive papier-mâché Easter Island head, while Tony staked torches with crepe-paper flames about the yard.

"I been rethinking that raise," Ernie said.

"Rethink it? We had a deal!" Swimming Pool snapped.

"What deal? This was no deal," Ernie asserted.

Over Swimming Pool's shoulder, Ernie saw a whole pack of hula dancers, both boys and girls, as they arrived in grass skirts at the gate.

"We shook hands! I get a raise!" Swimming Pool argued. "A raise, a raise, a raise."

"Whoa, whoa, whoa," Ernie protested. "This was no deal. I remember the 'talk about.' You said, 'In six weeks we talk about a raise.' I don't remember the deal."

"So start talking," said Swimming Pool. She dug her heels in the dirt and threw her hands on her hips.

"Now is not the time, Swimming Pool," said Ernie, jabbing a thumb toward the newly arrived guests. Hula dancers were already descended on the yard with a boom box blasting Hawaiian music, full of happy ukuleles and bongos.

Betty followed quickly on the hula dancers' heels, wearing an elaborate Polynesian headdress. With her free hand, she draped floral leis around Dusty and Tony as though she'd just been voted Head Hula Girl. "My story is about the mountains," she said in lilting musical tones, "and the turtle that came from the sea."

"Ernie," Swimming Pool protested, "you promised me a raise!"

"Now is not the time," Ernie repeated, "so keep your voice down and get to work!"

Swimming Pool didn't care who was listening.

"Oh, no! I bet it's not the time!" she shouted over the music. "It's never the right time when you have to stick up for yourself."

Ernie gestured helplessly at the crazy scene unfolding in the yard. "Bad timing, Pool," he said. "Funeral's starting! We'll talk later." Then he ran for cover behind Dusty on the other side of the cemetery.

Swimming Pool watched Ernie run away, muttered, "Of all the greedy, no-good . . . ," and took off after him.

She would have caught Ernie right away, but Betty rushed up to her full of Polynesian goodwill. "I have a grass skirt for you, Swimming Pool!" Betty said in a singsong voice with lots of enthusiasm.

"I don't think so," Swimming Pool groused as she ducked Betty's arm and stormed after Ernie.

Across the yard, Dusty was pushing a cumbersome grocery cart onto the grass. He had laced the prongs of the grocery cart with strips of blue fabric to suggest the sea. Inside the grocery cart was a liter soda bottle painted dark green to look like an oxygen tank. And inside the oxygen tank was Polynesian Pete the Turtle.

"Dusty!" Ernie cried. "You are not burying a grocery cart! A grocery cart for a turtle!" Ernie was flabbergasted.

"It's symbolic!" Dusty argued. "Returning Pete to the great big ocean."

Ernie had had just about enough argument for one day. "Flush him down the toilet!" he shouted. "He'll get there twice as fast."

Swimming Pool dodged through the hula dancers to get to Ernie. Just when she thought she was in the clear, she ran into Tony, cradling a hefty science-fair project. "Hey, Castellano!" Tony hollered. "Where do you want the volcano?"

Swimming Pool ducked under the volcano to get right into Ernie's face. "I'm not taking no for an answer, Ernie!" she snapped.

"Hold it! Everybody just hold it!" Ernie shouted, much louder than he had even intended—and everything went silent.

"That's better," Ernie commented—and he switched into quick-decision mode. Turning to Dusty, he said, "Nix the grocery cart. And the oxygen tank. And bury Polynesian Pete in the volcano."

"I like it!" Dusty enthused. Dusty snagged the liter bottle containing Pete and gave the grocery cart a little kick.

Tony clumsily handed him the volcano. "Careful," Tony warned, "it's loaded."

"Tony, where's your shovel?" Ernie asked.

"In the shed."

"We need a hole for the volcano, Tony. Don't you think you should dig it?"

"Sure thing, Castellano." Tony ran to retrieve his shovel.

Swimming Pool was still waiting to discuss her

133

salary—and her patience was wearing thin.

"All right, then," Ernie sighed. "Swimming Pool . . . "

Ernie was about to face Swimming Pool and deal with the problem—but Finny and Fanny, the designated mourners, arrived on the scene. They were dressed in identical white sarongs, with big, red fake hibiscus blooms tucked behind their ears. They were wild-eyed with excitement. They jumped in front of Ernie, positively giddy, and cried, "Ernie, Ernie! Where do we stand?"

Swimming Pool tried to elbow Finny and Fanny out of the way to command Ernie's attention. "Ernie, I want my raise. Give me that raise or I walk."

"Oh, what—you're threatening me now?"

It had become a shouting match between them now—and everybody was listening. It was like a Ping-Pong contest, full of lots of "You'll be sorry's" and "I told you so's." It went back and forth for several rounds until it came down to the whammy that made all the kids gasp.

"You wanna get fired, Swimming Pool, is that what you want?"

"You can't fire me, I *quit!*"

That was when all the kids gasped. Dusty gasped. Finny and Fanny gasped. Polynesian Betty looked like she was in a state of shock.

And no one was more surprised than Swimming Pool. The words had just come out of her mouth.

She had said it without thinking. But it felt so good to say, she had no regrets.

"You can't fire Swimming Pool!" Finny protested.

Swimming Pool hooted contemptuously. "Oh, no! Too late! I'm quitting! I'm *outta here*," she declared. She turned to storm out of the yard, but Finny and Fanny blocked her path.

"Swimming Pool! Our little Polynesian Pete!" Finny and Fanny cried.

Still not thinking, Swimming Pool snapped, "Sorry, girls, I'm not so crushed about your stinking squashed turtle!"

The gasp factor went up a notch after that little remark. Nobody had ever heard Swimming Pool address the bereaved in such a disrespectful manner. Even Swimming Pool felt a little ashamed this time. *Everything is whirling horribly out of control*, she thought, *but there doesn't seem to be any way to stop it.*

Ironically, Ernie was having the exact same thought. *It's all whacked and out of control*, he thought. And there didn't seem to be any stopping it now. Ernie had his reputation to consider. And he had to save face in front of the other kids.

"All right, then, go! Go already!" Ernie retorted. "Good luck finding another job!"

"I don't need another job. I'm going into business for myself!" Swimming Pool declared.

Ernie laughed haughtily. "You? Business? Don't make me laugh. You're a crier for hire, Swimming

Pool. Business? You don't have what it takes."

Swimming Pool tried to push through the hula dancers, but she ran straight into Tony with his great big shovel. Swimming Pool seized the shovel and thrust it at Ernie. "Here you go, Ernie," she said with enormous self-satisfaction. "Take this job and shove it."

Ernie staggered backward under the unexpected weight of the shovel. Meanwhile, Swimming Pool turned on her heel and stormed out of the yard, stumbling clumsily over the vacillating sprinkler head on the way. She scrambled to her feet, brushed off her knees, threw her head back with dignity, and left the cemetery altogether.

"Swimming Pool!" Ernie called after her, but he was already falling backward with the shovel. Before he could recover his balance, Ernie bumped into the grocery cart. The grocery cart skittered across the yard and careened into the hula dancers, who collided with the tiki god, which toppled onto the volcano, which provoked some kind of baking-soda eruption. The volcano shuddered, trembled, and finally erupted, spewing a homemade baking-soda recipe of foam across the yard.

Finny, Fanny, and Betty burst into screams. Yelping and squealing, the hula dancers ran for cover in a flurry of grass skirts. Each hula boy and hula girl ran pell-mell in crazy patterns about the yard, so that they ended up colliding in one horrible clump.

Across the alley, Swimming Pool tripped over the green garden hose that stretched back to Dusty's toolshed, and scraped her knee again in the process. She found the spigot and gave the faucet a sharp twist.

Naturally, after that there was suddenly a deluge of water-water-everywhere in the cemetery. The water pressure was so high that the sprinkler head snaked into a frenzied Water Wiggle and spritzed all over the kids' heads. Of course, the screams got louder and the collisions got worse and the whole place just turned into bedlam. Finny and Fanny were beside themselves. Their tranquil South Seas funeral had turned into a hurricane.

In the middle of this chaos, Ernie and Dusty bonked heads in the center of the yard. The Water Wiggle seemed to have arrived out of nowhere like a giant anaconda, and it wrapped around them, tighter and tighter. The children screamed, the volcano erupted, and the deluge continued to flow.

Calamity reigned.

Chapter Twenty-three

Life Without Swimming Pool

All the whiny hula dancers had finally cleared the yard, trailing their soggy grass skirts behind them. Finny and Fanny had agreed to reschedule their turtle burial for a time when the ground wasn't quite so muddy.

And Ernie and Dusty were left alone in the yard to survey the damage. Nothing was too much the worse for wear, except that the papier-mâché volcano had pretty much turned to mulch.

"Time for cleanup," Ernie grumbled.

"At least the flowers got a good watering," Dusty enthused.

Ernie shot him a look that said, "I don't wanna hear about the bright side."

Dusty started gathering up the discarded floral leis in the grass. "We're not really losing

Swimming Pool, are we, Boss?" he asked.

"We're not losing Swimming Pool," Ernie announced. "She'll come around."

Dusty was relieved. Swimming Pool gave the business a lot of heart. "It'll be good to have Swimming Pool back," he said to Ernie. He didn't mention that the business without Swimming Pool wasn't anything Dusty wanted to imagine. That's why Dusty gulped hard when he heard Ernie utter one more word.

Ernie had stepped to the center of the yard and looked around at the wet everything. And the word he said was, "Although . . ."

"What are you thinking, Boss?"

Ernie flipped a hand in the air, as though he was weighing the possibility of what he was thinking. "It's not like she's not replaceable," he said.

"You gonna replace Swimming Pool, Boss?"

"Cry. Sob. Boo-hoo," Ernie mocked. "Who couldn't do that? I'll put an ad up at Miss Ginger's School of Tap and Tumbling. Bound to be a few crybabies in there. When Swimming Pool sees she's got some competition, she'll come running. You wait and see."

"Boss," Dusty ventured, "I don't think that's such a good idea."

"You got a better idea, Dusty?" Ernie snapped. And then he added, "You like your job, Dusty?"

Dusty flinched. "You wouldn't fire me, would you, Boss?"

"I'm just looking for a little support. That's all,"

Ernie said. Nice enough. But it sounded like a warning.

Swimming Pool got home and immediately started thinking of all the things she should have said. *I should have asked him why people like his crummy business in the first place*, she thought. And the answer in her mind was, *Me*.

But then, of course, Swimming Pool was distracted by thoughts of remorse. She had no idea where she stood, and she was full of self-doubts. "What have I done?" she asked herself. "I didn't have a deal in writing. All I wanted was a raise. I didn't mean to quit the job altogether."

Everything was falling apart and she felt like it was all her fault.

Swimming Pool groaned and buried her head in a pillow. She almost didn't hear the jingle of the ice-cream truck outside. But when the jingle managed to penetrate through the pillow, Swimming Pool thought an orange Popsicle might just be the thing to cheer her up. So she threw herself off the bed and headed downstairs.

And what am I supposed to do now? she thought, still miserable, as she headed for the curb. *I gotta start a business for myself? How am I ever going to launch a business for myself?*

Fortunately, Swimming Pool ran into Tony hanging out by the back end of the ice-cream truck.

"Hey. Kid with the shovel," she said.

"Name's Tony," he snapped, not one to suffer fools gladly. Tony was coping with a Sno-Caps ice-cream cone that was melting all over his fist.

"I know that," said Swimming Pool. "I was just trying to be funny. Hey, kid with the shovel named Tony. You still working for Ernie?"

Tony shrugged. "Course I am," he said. "I'll work for anybody. Keeps me in ice-cream cones. I get paid to shovel. It's not complicated. When I got a gig, I gotta dig. That's my motto. I'm an independent contractor."

Swimming Pool had never heard the expression before. "Independent what? What's that?"

"Independent contractor," Tony repeated. "Got a nice ring, don't it? I just get in there, do the job, get paid, and get out."

Swimming Pool ordered her orange Popsicle and joined Tony on the curb.

"Independent contractor. You got the life," she said.

Tony leaned on his shovel and slurped off the bottom of his cone. "Yeah, I'm a free agent. In business for *myself.*"

"My brother's an independent contractor," Swimming Pool asserted. She was thinking of her runaway brother, Rick. "He's got a band." Rick had this garage band he played in sometimes. Every now and then, they got a paying gig and Rick would be all excited.

"Is that right?"

141

"Well, sometimes he's a busboy and he's hourly plus tips—but when he's a drummer with the band, he's an independent contractor—like you. That's the life. No haggling over a salary. Just get in there, do the job, get paid, and get out."

"I was lucky," Tony said. He laid his shovel down on the grass to wipe his fingers with a crumpled napkin. "See, I had this shovel. Ernie asked me to dig a hole. And I dug it. It's a simple story. Other people saw the shovel, saw the hole, liked what they saw. Asked me if I could come over and dig at their house. Lots of uses for a hole in the ground. That's why you gotta diversify."

"Diversi-what?"

"Dig anything. One day, a dead canary; another day, a rosebush. I dig whatever people pay fifty cents for me to dig."

"You are very smart."

"It's not smart. It's moxie. Find something you can do and do it well. Let people know you can do it. And ask for money. That's how you get into business for yourself."

Business for myself, thought Swimming Pool. She paused to ponder this piece of information. *Maybe I can make this work.*

"Thanks, Tony. You really dug me out of a jam," she said, and got up off the curb to head back inside.

"Whoa, ma'am," Tony said. He held out a sticky palm. "That'll be fifty cents, please."

• • •

Ernie was exhausted. He'd made a lot of decisions in the course of one single day and his head hurt. Even so, he'd promised Mister Doggie, and he couldn't break his promise.

Ernie opened the window in his bedroom and hitched his legs onto the windowsill. Mister Doggie was zipped inside Ernie's windbreaker, and he rustled uneasily as Ernie negotiated the ledge.

"It's okay, Doggie," Ernie said. "Almost there."

Ernie skittered onto the shingled roof outside the window. He was trying to be quiet because he wasn't really supposed to be out here. He settled on the shingles and unzipped his windbreaker. Mister Doggie stuck his nose through the gap to see what was going on.

"Okay, Doggie, look up." Ernie pointed above to the stars in the night sky. "The Big Dipper. See? Like an ice-cream scoop." It was a clear night and the Big Dipper was easy to spot. "And there's the Little Dipper," he said when he'd tracked that constellation down in the sky. "It's like a scoop, only smaller. Like for melon balls."

Mister Doggie settled more comfortably onto Ernie's lap, and Ernie stretched his legs out for better balance. "One of these constellations is supposed to be a doggie. I wrote a report on it once. But I forget." Mister Doggie seemed satisfied enough with the Big and Little Dippers. "So that's the nighttime world," Ernie said. "The world of the stars."

Mister Doggie squirmed inside Ernie's jacket.

"You've seen the basement and here's the rooftop. And that's about all of the world you get."

There was a night chill in the air. Ernie cuddled closer to the dog in his arms, more for the warmth than anything else. "Mom brought us up here once—but you were still little. You probably forget. I remember though. That night with the stars."

Mister Doggie whimpered slightly and squirmed in his arms. "You cold, Mister Doggie?" Ernie asked. "You cold, or you just want to cuddle?"

Mister Doggie pressed his ear to Ernie's chest as though he was listening to his windup clock. When Ernie peeked inside his windbreaker, he saw that Mister Doggie's eyes were closed.

Ernie could have gone back inside. But he decided to stay a while longer and check out the stars.

Chapter Twenty-four

Business for Herself

The science fair took up the entire gymnasium floor.

There were quite a few volcanoes this year. And then the usual roster of marigold experiments, dinosaur exhibits, and meteorological charts. But there was one rather unique exhibit—situated down the third aisle, right in the middle of the gym.

Swimming Pool was an exhibit all by herself. She sat on a stool under a poster that read, CRYBABY: THE SODIUM CONTENT OF TEARS.

Gina positioned her microscope on the card table and turned crisply to address three judges from the school faculty. "I intend to quantify the sodium content of tears at the very moment they are shed," she announced. With that said, she extended a microscope slide to scoop a teardrop gingerly from Pool's cheek—only there was one problem.

Swimming Pool was not crying.

Gina smiled apologetically at the judges. "One moment, please," she said, and turned toward Swimming Pool.

"What's with the tears, Pool?" Gina said between gritted teeth. "You promised me tears."

"But what am I supposed to cry about?" Swimming Pool asked.

Gina clutched her clipboard to her chest and pushed a pencil through her braid. "Um. This is science. I pay for the tears; I don't need to know where you got 'em. Understood?"

Swimming Pool sighed. "Gimme a moment, okay, Gina? I'll get you some tears." Gina arched a dubious eyebrow and turned back to explain her thesis to the judges.

Swimming Pool was stumped. Ever since she'd gone into business for herself, the jobs had gotten stranger and stranger. She had been asked to stage temper tantrums during math tests and crying jags in grocery stores. It was kind of humiliating. At first, Swimming Pool took any job that came along. But she was becoming more and more suspect of the jobs that compromised her sense of propriety.

I just don't feel appreciated, Swimming Pool thought. She sulked as she sat there, wondering where she was going to find the tears for Gina's science fair project and generally feeling worse by the minute about this unfortunate turn in her crying career, when who should appear but Dusty. He was down by the dinosaurs at the end of the third aisle. And he was headed her way.

"Hey, Dusty," she said.

"Pool. Long time no," Dusty said with a smile, as though it had been years.

Dusty held out his hand, and Swimming Pool understood his mission. She reached into her pocket and passed him the routine wad of bills. "Thanks for doing this, Dusty," she said.

"No problem," Dusty answered. "How's business?"

"A little strange, but going okay." She avoided mentioning the bad gigs she'd been asked to work— and the bizarre circumstances that had landed her a gig during the middle of the science fair. "Miss me much?" Swimming Pool asked.

Dusty couldn't answer that question. Instead he spoke rapidly, and it all came out in a rush. "It hasn't been the same without you. Business is awful. We're just barely getting by. Ernie's a wreck. Swimming Pool, we need you back."

"I don't know, Dusty," Swimming Pool hedged. "You got more patience than I do. You got more patience than anyone I know."

"Patience is a virtue."

"You can handle Ernie," she said. "You can. Not me."

"What can I say? I got a high threshold for

pain—and art is my life. But we both miss you, Swimming Pool. He won't say it, but I will." There was nothing Swimming Pool could say to that. So Dusty kept going. "Talk to him, Pool. He's stubborn and thick skulled and he sure knows how to squeeze a dollar, but, you know, he's not a bad kid. You should talk to him."

Swimming Pool crossed her arms. "I talked to him plenty. He needs to talk to me. He needs to apologize."

Dusty couldn't argue that point. So he tried a different approach. "Did you hear about Mister Doggie?" he asked, changing the subject.

"Ernie's dog we're not supposed to know anything about?" Swimming Pool asked.

"Yeah. Not feeling so—"

Swimming Pool held out her hand. "No. Don't tell me."

Dusty crammed his hands in his pockets. "Could be nothing. Just getting old."

"Yeah, well. Poor Doggie. I hope so."

Dusty didn't say anything else after that. He just shrugged and walked away.

Swimming Pool watched Dusty disappear down the aisle and suddenly started feeling nostalgic for the good old days. It was almost like being homesick even. But she didn't get to feel homesick for long, because Gina intruded on the moment. "Swimming Pool," she said, a little testy and impatient.

"Okay. One second, Gina," said Swimming

Pool, feeling just a little bit misty-eyed. "Almost there."

When Dusty stopped by the mall that afternoon, he swung by Rick's guitar case to drop off another wad of bills. Only this time, the moment the wad landed in the guitar case, Rick jumped up from the pavement and tried to grab Dusty's arm.

"Hey, kid!" said Rick.

Dusty wrenched his arm free and started to run. Little kids can often run really fast through a crowd of grown people. Not that Rick actually tried to chase him down.

But while Dusty was dodging through the crowd, he did hear Rick's voice. He was yelling, "I just wanna talk to you! I just wanna ask you about Swimming Pool!"

Uh-oh, thought Dusty. *I blew it.* If Rick was mentioning Swimming Pool's name to him, then Rick had figured everything out. And Dusty was going to have to tell Swimming Pool that he probably couldn't do the drop anymore.

Everything was falling apart. And Dusty felt like it was entirely his fault.

Chapter Twenty-five

Boys Don't Cry

Ernie held auditions for a new crier on a Saturday afternoon. About fifteen kids stood in a row across the grassy part of the cemetery. Dusty and Ernie perched on top of the picnic table as the lineup of kids ran through enough squeaks, gulps, and "wah's" to fill a calliope.

"My turtle bit me on the lip, so my mom said we had to put him to . . . ," one timid little girl declared in a big, booming voice.

"I tried to feed her a little milk with an eye-dropper. It just rolled off her cheek!" wailed a little boy.

"I called out, 'Cupcake, Cupcake, Cupcake!'"

"He looked up. And shuddered. And wiggled his little ears."

"His tail was still moving!"

"'Speak to me! Speak to me! Speak to me!'"

Of course, they were all crying, crying, crying. It was pretty hysterical.

When it was all over and the auditionees had finally left the yard, Ernie said, "Well, that didn't go too badly."

Dusty hooted. "Are you kidding me?" he cried. Dusty let out a high, shrill shriek. It was an elaborate imitation of all the worst audition performances—and there were more bad than good.

Dusty and Ernie doubled over with laughter. And pretty soon, they were rolling in the grass.

"How about the one who sounded like air leaking out of a balloon?" Ernie howled, and imitated the high-pitched whine.

"Or the one who sounded like a rusty swing set," Dusty said, screeching back and forth in a snivel.

"Or that blubber that sounded like a clogged drain!"

"Or the garbage truck with the backing-beeper!"

Ernie and Dusty laughed and laughed as they imitated all the worst of the crybabies. But when their laughter finally died down and they lay there gasping for breath, Dusty's voice shifted into a wail of despair.

"We got to get Swimming Pool back, Boss!" Dusty urged.

Ernie was adamant. "We don't gotta get Swimming Pool."

"But we looked at ten girls and five boys today, and they were all a disaster!"

"We'll try Wendy," Ernie announced. "I said I'd turn this business around, and I will."

"Wendy!" Dusty cried. He perched his hands by his ears like a great big mouse and went, "Squeak, squeak!" It was a very good imitation of Wendy in action.

"Wendy had a lot of enthusiasm," Ernie insisted.

"Boss, she's a cheerleader!" Dusty did the thing with his ears again—and added a mock set of pom-poms to his impersonation. "Squeak, squeak!" he chimed, like a mouse at a pep rally.

Ernie wasn't impressed.

"Swimming Pool has *sincerity*," Dusty pleaded. "You can't put a dollar sign on sincerity."

"I'll hang a dollar sign on Wendy and she'll work out just fine," Ernie argued. "I can get this business out of the hole. Heck, if Wendy's not right for the job—I'll do it myself!"

Dusty was about to gasp, "Boss, you're not considering . . ."

Before he could get it out, Ernie had already grabbed his hand and was attempting a genuine *whimper*. It wasn't bad as whimpers go. In fact, Ernie did a pretty good job. Gaining confidence in his ability, Ernie went ahead and added a few little yelps to the whimper. Ernie nodded with satisfaction. "I'm not half bad at this," he said, and began blubbering louder still.

"Nice try, Boss," Dusty said, "but, you'll forgive me, it doesn't seem altogether . . . sincere."

"I can do sincere," Ernie insisted. He wrapped an arm around Dusty's shoulder and added louder sobs to the whimper.

"Well, perhaps, Boss," Dusty allowed. "But still a little lacking in the compassion department."

"I can do compassion," Ernie insisted. He grabbed both of Dusty's hands and bellowed louder still. He petted Dusty as if he were a dog. He sniffled and sniveled and shook his head like it was all such a crying shame.

Dusty suffered through Ernie's performance with a poker face.

When it got about as embarrassing as it could possibly get, they heard a voice say, "Have I come at a bad time?"

Ernie and Dusty both jumped. Swimming Pool was standing at the edge of the yard. And there was no telling how long she'd been standing there.

Dusty took the opportunity to hop over the picnic table. On the one hand, he couldn't wait to hear what was going to happen. On the other hand, he'd rather be anywhere but here. Dusty wasn't very good with confrontations.

"I better fire up the old hot-glue gun," he said. "The Quart-Size Cracker Barrel for Corky's Chameleon. Hey, that's hard to say. You'll excuse me." Dusty grabbed his suitcase, ran through the gate, and zipped across the alley.

Ernie and Swimming Pool found themselves alone in the cemetery. It was just like old times.

"So. Hello, Ernie," she said, perching on the picnic table.

"Hello, *traitor.*"

"That's not fair. I came by to talk to you like friends."

Ernie scoffed. "Friends? Sure, friends. Not like me to carry a grudge. How you been, Swimming Pool. Heard you went into business for yourself."

"Good to hear I'm getting a little word of mouth."

"Sounds like business is good."

"Going great. Not complaining."

"Good to hear. *Traitor.*"

This wasn't going the way Swimming Pool had planned. "Ernie, I didn't stop by to fight," Swimming Pool said. "I only came by because we used to have a good thing going here, Ernie."

Ernie sat on the other end of the picnic table. "Okay, okay," he said. "What's on your mind?"

Swimming Pool was on the spot. "Ernie," she began, "I know it's over between us. I don't work for you anymore. You got no reason to be listening to me. But I liked working for you, Ernie. I had a good time with you and Dusty."

"Uh-huh," he said. "And . . ." Like she should get to the point.

Swimming Pool sighed. "Ernie, you don't understand," she continued. "That work was hard."

"You're a hard worker. I thought you liked working hard."

"I do. I did," Swimming Pool insisted. "I am a hard worker. But I left thinking you didn't appreciate me. I don't think you did appreciate me."

Ernie scoffed. "I appreciated you plenty."

Swimming Pool jabbed her finger to show she was finally making her point. "Then you should have taken better care of me. You promised me a raise."

Ernie shrugged. "'Business is business.'" And he did that finger gesture that Principal Bridwell did for quotation marks.

"Ugh," Swimming Pool said in disgust. "You made me a promise and you reneged. Friends don't do that to friends."

Ernie got off the picnic table to protest. "Is this about business or is this about friends?"

"Both maybe, maybe both. I was your friend. We were a team."

"Hey!" Ernie argued. "You walked. You even went out and started your own business. Let's get that straight. I didn't fire you; you walked."

"You weren't taking care of me. I had to take care of myself."

"Okay, then"—Ernie shrugged as though the matter was settled—"we all gotta take care of ourselves."

"You should take better care of the people who work for you," Swimming Pool asserted.

Ernie smirked. "Dusty doesn't complain," he said.

"Dusty's a shy guy and he does good work. Just

'cause he doesn't stand up to you and he's got a high threshold for pain—that doesn't mean he doesn't complain."

Ernie scoffed. "What do you know? Dusty and I are a team."

Swimming Pool felt a tirade coming on. "I was on that team, and it didn't always feel like a team," she shouted. "And you could still have me on that team if you'd treated me better!"

Ernie smiled just a little too smugly. "You want your job back!" he said, as though he had just figured out the reason for Swimming Pool's visit. "Is that what this is all about? You want your old job back, Swimming Pool?"

Swimming Pool couldn't answer that question. She was too angry with Ernie at the moment even to think straight.

Ernie pulled his cell phone out of his pocket. "Give me a moment, would you, Swimming Pool?" he said as he dialed a number. While it rang, he held his hand over the mouthpiece and said to Swimming Pool, "This will just take a second."

Swimming Pool folded her arms and studied Ernie. He was up to something and she knew it.

It didn't take long to find out what.

"Wendy!" Ernie cried into the phone with just a trace too much glee.

"Wendy?" Swimming Pool repeated.

Ernie perked up on the telephone. "Good news! You're hired!"

"That little squirrel on Pee-Wee Cheerleading?" Swimming Pool sneered.

Ernie covered the mouthpiece with one hand. "That little squirrel has a lot of enthusiasm," he answered back.

Swimming Pool put her hands behind her ears and wagged them like a great big mouse. "Squeak, squeak," she said.

"What are you complaining about? The way I hear it, you're doing business hand over—" Ernie pulled his hand away from the phone and spoke into it with enthusiasm. "Yeah, Wendy, you start tomorrow! . . . Oh, I'm looking forward to it too. Oops— can you hold a moment? I've got another call."

Ernie shrugged at Swimming Pool, as though the phone was ringing off the hook these days. He clicked over to the other call while Swimming Pool stewed.

"Ernie here," he announced, smiling happily in Swimming Pool's direction. "Annie! What can I do ya? Ant farm bit the dust? Gee, those were sweet ants. Each one such a *hard worker*."

Swimming Pool got up from the picnic table and brushed off her jeans. "Wendy!" she snapped one final time.

When Ernie looked up, Swimming Pool was gone.

Chapter Twenty-six

Squeak, Squeak

Wendy was a pint-size cheerleader, and what she lacked in stature, she made up for in enthusiasm. In fact, Wendy was known for her school spirit. She was also decidedly shrill.

During the services for a small lizard named Louie, Wendy marched in giant strides to the center of the yard with two large, black crepe-paper pompoms. Summoning great authority, she began shouting with all her might at Ernie and Dusty and the few mourners who had gathered in the yard.

"Give me a *W!*" Wendy shouted.

"*W,*" the tiny congregation responded, somewhat wary and confused.

"Give me an *A!*" Wendy shouted.

The congregation looked a little more confused. Wendy only took the spelling lesson up to *H*. And once the congregation had doubtfully spelled out "*W-A-H,*" Wendy started doing handstands and cartwheels all over the yard as she chirped, "Wah, wah, wah-wah-wah! Wah-wah-wah, wah! Let's go!"

The cheer repeated itself two or three times, with unflagging energy. Ernie found himself ducking the occasional pom-pom as Wendy threw herself through her enthusiastic drill. She finished the routine with a roundoff, a standing split, and a big, triumphant smile.

The mourners looked askance. There was a smattering of applause, but they didn't hang around long after the burial was completed. Dusty smugly turned to study Ernie's reaction. Ernie hung his head in shame. This had been a bad call.

Dusty tried to bring the subject up as though it was no big deal. "Can we bring Swimming Pool back now, Boss?"

"No!" Ernie barked. "No Swimming Pool! She embarrassed me in front of my clientele! She mocked me in front of everybody! No Swimming Pool. I got my pride, you know!"

Usually Dusty didn't try to talk to Ernie when he was angry. When Ernie was fired up, he didn't listen to anybody and he didn't like to be interrupted. This time, Dusty spoke up despite himself. "I'm proud of you, Ernie," Dusty said. "None of this would have been possible without you."

"I've had it with this talk about Swimming Pool. I don't want to hear any more about Swimming Pool."

"But Swimming Pool is the heart of this operation!"

"You like your job, Dusty?" Ernie said with that warning edge in his voice.

"I love my job," Dusty said. "You know I love my job. But it's no good throwing funerals without Swimming Pool! It's just a waste of good business!"

"Don't tell me what's good for business!" Ernie hollered. "I know what's good for business!" He stamped around the yard, huffing and puffing. "This is my business! I built this business from nothing! I turned this business around before, and I'll turn it around again! This is my business!"

Dusty tried to get a word in edgewise, but there was no interrupting Ernie once he got all righteous and indignant and huffy about business.

Everything was falling apart. Totally exasperated, Dusty slammed his hands against his ears to try to drown it out. But it was no good. He couldn't watch Ernie destroy the business. He couldn't watch the cemetery go down the drain. And he just couldn't listen to it anymore.

Dusty jumped on top of the picnic table and whacked the wind chime hanging from the tree. Dusty whacked it hard enough to knock it off the branch. The wind chime fell through the air, clanking and clattering and making a horrible sound, until it landed with a *thump* in the grass, suddenly mute.

It was the distraction of silence that finally got Ernie's attention. He looked up to find Dusty standing on top of the picnic table, red faced and near tears.

"It's not the business we were trying to save!" Dusty shouted, so upset he couldn't even see straight. "Haven't you figured that out? It never was the stinking business!"

Ernie looked blankly at Dusty as though he was a wild man.

Dusty jumped off the table and ran out of the yard. Ernie stayed behind, appearing rather concerned and embarrassed. He was also feeling kind of abandoned and alone.

It occurred to Ernie that he was standing alone in the yard for maybe the first time since he'd discovered the place. *Everything is falling apart*, he thought. But he couldn't figure out why. "This can't be my fault," he said to himself.

Sure enough, just as he looked like a complete idiot talking to himself, Ernie heard a voice call out his name.

"Ernie?"

Ernie jumped. A figure with a shopping bag and a flashlight moved into the yard.

Cat Lady stepped forward where he could see her.

"Dang, Cat Lady. You scared me."

Cat Lady stumbled awkwardly and spoke with a certain difficulty. "It's Catherine. And I'm sorry. The kids told me I might find you . . . I need your services. For my cat."

It was only then that Ernie noticed Cat Lady had been crying.

"Your cat?" he asked timidly. "Um, which one?"

"#62," Cat Lady replied. "You met him. The fat tabby one . . ."

"With the boots. And the whiskers."

"Yes, his boots. If it's not too inconvenient, can I ask you to, you know . . . would you bury him for me? This cemetery is such a beautiful place. And I've decided that this is where I want #62 to be." Cat Lady held up her shopping bag. It bulged with #62. Ernie did a double take.

"I guess that would be all right."

"Let's go, then."

She handed the bag to Ernie. It was heavier than you'd think.

"Don't worry. He's wrapped up in a towel like a mummy. Quite sanitary."

Ernie grabbed the potting tool they'd used to plant all the flowers and dug a shallow grave for Cat #62. It wasn't too difficult to do. Cat Lady sat on the piano bench under the trestle. "We put it there for people who need quiet reflection," Ernie had explained. And Cat Lady had said, "Thank you."

Dusk was settling in on the yard, and Ernie was pushing the time he was due home and at the dinner table. But he figured he had a priority going here with Cat Lady and Cat #62.

"You're sure this is no trouble?" Cat Lady had asked.

"Gotcha covered, Cat Lady. Don't you worry about a thing," Ernie had said.

Unfortunately, it was soon nightfall in the cemetery. By the time the hole was dug, the grave site was barely visible in the moonlight. Ernie and Cat Lady had to bury Cat #62 by flashlight.

"You might want to mark it with gravel, if you like," Ernie suggested.

"I'd like that very much." Cat Lady decorated the gravesite with a small pattern of gravel and then patted it with a kiss. She stood up and discreetly tucked Ernie's fee into his shirt pocket.

"Thank you for the services."

"You're welcome, Cat Lady."

Cat Lady brushed herself off. "You do a wonderful job here, Ernie," she declared. "You should be very proud."

"Yeah, well, unfortunately it looks like you might have just gotten the last funeral we're gonna have here anytime soon."

Cat Lady looked concerned. "Why's that?" she asked.

"I had a little staff mutiny," Ernie said, hedging on the absolute truth.

"Mutiny?" Cat Lady asked.

"They all either quit or got fired," he said, which was closer to the truth. "And business has been going downhill. So maybe it's time to just let the business fold."

Cat Lady patted Ernie gently on the shoulder.

163

"Well, I'm very sorry to hear that," she said. "You ran a good business, Ernie." She picked up her empty shopping bag and they headed toward the gate. "But more than that," she added, "you built something bigger. Something special. Something more rare."

"What's that?" Ernie asked.

"You brought people together," Cat Lady replied.

Ernie mulled over that thought. And something was beginning to sink in.

Chapter Twenty-seven

Good-bye Sky, Good-bye Trees

Ernie was seriously late. He hustled home to the brownstone and slipped into the kitchen through the back door. At the very sound of the lock, Red called out from the den, "Ernie!"

Ernie saw an empty bucket of fried chicken on the kitchen counter and spotted a platter full of fried chicken on the dining-room table. Biscuits, mashed potatoes, and green beans. Ernie walked over to touch the platter, but it was all cold, cold, cold.

"Ernie! Look at the time!" Red shouted as he entered the dining room.

"Dad, I can explain," Ernie blurted out.

"No explanation! I've been worried sick! You could have been hit by a car. You could have been laid up in the hospital."

"I had a funeral, Dad."

Red clapped his hands together and wagged his fingers sternly in Ernie's face. "Don't you smart-mouth me, young man!"

"A funeral for Cat Lady, Dad!"

There. He had said it. Once it was out in the open, there was no way to keep it a secret. Ernie decided to come clean about the whole thing. "I been throwing pet funerals for kids in the neighborhood. I bury their dead pets." It actually felt good to set the record straight.

"Dead pets?" Red thought for a moment, and then somehow it all made sense. How Ernie had been so preoccupied all the time. The number of times he'd been late for supper. How Ernie had a gang of new friends around the house. And how that empty old lot down the alley had been spruced up, and how there were cupcakes and dog treats and cat toys lying in the grass. *Wait a minute*, he thought.

"In that empty old lot down the alley?" he asked out loud.

"It's not as empty as you'd think," Ernie replied.

"So . . . this was a business."

Ernie nodded.

"A business," Red repeated. "After I told you that you weren't allowed to start any more businesses?"

Ernie nodded.

"You're grounded," Red said flatly.

"Dad!" Ernie protested.

"What did I tell you would happen if you started another business? I said you'd be grounded.

And so you are. You are so grounded. Say good-bye sky and good-bye trees." Red waved both hands to punctuate the moral of the lesson. "Ernie, you've got to learn not to take advantage of people."

Ernie couldn't help but try to defend himself. "But I'm not taking advantage of people anymore, Dad. The business is over! It's finished! I promise it won't happen again."

"The business is finished?" Red asked suspiciously. "Just how long has this been going on?"

"About three months," Ernie replied.

"Three months!" Red barked. "That's it. I'm increasing the punishment."

"Dad, that's no fair!"

"You're grounded *and* you do the dishes."

This was ridiculous. "What dishes?" Ernie asked. "You never cook."

"Yeah, well, I do from now on," Red insisted.

"Dad, please," Ernie begged. "I've been punished enough already. Don't cook."

Red turned his head slightly at Ernie's snide joke—at any other time he would have thought it was funny. But this time he wanted to make the punishment stick. "I said grounded," he declared one last time. "Do you hear me? Grounded."

Later that evening, Red left the house to pick up milk for the morning. Ernie had been sulking for the better part of the hour. And now he didn't know what to do with his newly grounded self. He'd finished his homework and there was nothing on TV.

Ernie headed upstairs and flung himself onto his bed, still upset and angry. After a moment, he sat up. Something was strange. Where was Mister Doggie?

Ernie stepped into the hallway.

"Doggie? Mister Doggie?"

Ernie slipped downstairs to check under the sofa, but no Doggie. Ernie whistled, shook the dog biscuits, jiggled the dog toy, and rattled the food dish. Nothing. No Doggie.

Ernie walked down the hall to Red's bedroom. The windup clock was lying on the floor beside the bed. Ernie reached down to pick it up. As he stood, he noticed that there, curled into a quiet ball on what had been his mother's side of the bed, was Mister Doggie.

Ernie reached out to scratch Mister Doggie gently behind the ears, the way he liked. But Mister Doggie didn't move. He didn't even whimper.

Ernie's face slowly went blank with the realization that Mister Doggie was gone. He just looked at the dog, lying so quiet and still.

After a moment, he saddled up on the mattress alongside Mister Doggie with the windup clock still in his hand. He gave the clock a gentle crank—and held it to his ear.

Ticktock, it said, *ticktock*.

Ernie's lip trembled slightly and he let his head drop.

Chapter Twenty-eight

Shake It

Pool was up to the S in a game of "H-O-R-S-E."

She was shooting foul shots by herself at the basketball hoop in the driveway when the garage door suddenly lifted from behind.

Rick appeared on the other side of the door. He was hauling a snare drum under one arm and raising the door with the other.

"Hey, Splish-Splash. How you doing?" he said.

"Not you again," Swimming Pool moaned.

"Mom and Dad weren't home, so I stopped by to claim my drums." He used his free hand to scoop a paper bag from the ground and stepped out into the sunlight.

Swimming Pool stopped dribbling and propped the ball against her hip. "Claiming your drums?" she said. "Guess that means you're never coming back."

"Water Wiggle, I'm gone and I been gone. You know that. You're looking at me—and I'm not even here."

"Then why you got to go?" Swimming Pool begged. "I'll understand. I promise I'll understand." She covered her face. She was not going to cry.

Rick put the drum down on the ground and reached to tug on Swimming Pool's sweatshirt. He was trying to comfort her, but he had never been really good at this sort of thing. "Come on, don't," he said. "Mmmarco. Mmmarco. Come on, say it. Marco . . ."

"Polo," Swimming Pool muttered from behind her hand.

Rick tapped her head affectionately. "There, you said it," he said.

Swimming Pool pushed his hand away. "Quit it. It hurts," she said.

"I wasn't hurting you," Rick protested.

"You always are," Swimming Pool said. "Every time I see you, I'm always saying good-bye."

Now Rick really felt like a heel. "Things change when you grow up, Swimming Pool. The world gets bigger. I'll be around if you need me. Don't be crying about it."

"I'm not crying about it," Swimming Pool protested. "I'm just warming up. I got this stinking job. I get paid to be upset about stuff."

"You cry?" Rick scoffed. "You hate to cry."

"Yeah, well, those are the breaks," Swimming

Pool concluded as she wiped at her cheeks with the back of her sleeve.

"High Dive, when you gonna listen to me? A job is just a job. Save yourself for you. Save your tears for when you really need 'em."

Rick threw a quick hug around Swimming Pool—fond, but roughhouse. Mushy stuff made both of them uncomfortable. He reached for his snare drum but paused to toss the paper sack at Swimming Pool. He did it like it was an afterthought or something. "Think fast!" Rick barked.

Swimming Pool caught the bag. "What is it?" she asked.

"Something to remember me by," said Rick. "Give it a shake. You'll see. Give it a shake and think of me."

Swimming Pool followed Rick down the driveway. When he climbed into the van, she jumped up to hang off the shotgun window on the passenger side.

"Gonna miss you, Rick," she said. "I know you say you'll be around and all, but still I'm gonna miss you."

Rick looked at the steering wheel because he was getting embarrassed. All this mushy stuff.

He didn't know how to tell Swimming Pool that he knew about the money. That he knew what she'd been doing for him. He didn't know how to say thank you and have it not sound mushy. But in the end, all he had was words.

171

So he said it anyway. "Thank you, Swimming Pool. I know what you did for me."

He was talking about the money, and Swimming Pool knew it, too. She broke into a slow-burning smirk. "Got you bad, didn't I?" she said.

Rick smiled too—and then he started the engine. Swimming Pool dropped to the sidewalk and slowly waved good-bye.

Rick called out across the seat, "Sharks and Minnows! Call me if you need me!" and pulled away from the curb. Swimming Pool was waving and she kept right on waving. She even walked out into the street and kept waving so that if Rick looked in the rearview mirror, all he would see was Swimming Pool waving good-bye.

When the van took the corner, Swimming Pool looked down at the paper bag in her other hand. She tugged it open and reached inside. It was a tambourine.

She flipped it over and raised it high. The tambourine rattled and shimmered as she shook it in the sun.

When Pool bounded into Dusty's toolshed calling, "Dusty, have you seen Ernie?" Dusty jumped to hide the suitcase project he was working on.

"Ernie?" Dusty asked. "You mean, you didn't hear?"

"Hear what?" Swimming Pool asked.

"About Mister Doggie?" said Dusty.

Swimming Pool went blank. "Oh, no," she said with a certain dread. "Don't tell me."

Dusty went back to his glue gun. "Okay," he said with a shrug.

"Dusty. Tell me!" Swimming Pool cried.

But when it came time to give the news, Dusty couldn't find the words. "Swimming Pool . . . ," he began. "Mister Doggie. What can I say?"

Chapter Twenty-nine

The Team Is Back

Ernie sat on his stoop with a box of tissues and a pair of sunglasses. The sunglasses were stupid, he knew—he just didn't want all the kids to see that he'd been crying. Swimming Pool came hauling around the corner and was about to take the steps two at a time and pound on Ernie's kitchen door, when she found him sitting on the steps. She just about tripped over her sneakers, but she caught her balance and stood at the bottom of the stairs, catching her breath.

"Ernie," she declared. "I came over as fast as I could. And I know this is totally bad timing—but you gotta hear me out."

It was a long windup for whatever she had to say. Ernie hitched his sunglasses down and peered over them at her.

"Say what's on your mind, Swimming Pool," he said.

Swimming Pool squared her shoulders and continued, "We can keep the business, Ernie. . . ."

Ernie moaned. "The business is gone, Pool. You were there—"

"But we can keep it alive," Swimming Pool cut him off. "Ernie, kids need you. You got a knack for coming up with . . . good business . . . that keeps kids together. And I will work for you, Ernie. Anytime, anywhere. But I have conditions." She ticked them off on her fingers. "Treat me fair." That was one finger. "Pay me what I'm worth." That was two fingers. "And if I do a good job, you gotta tell me I do a good job." She held the three fingers in the air to make it look simple and easy. "Deal?" she said as she wagged her fingers.

"Here are my conditions," Ernie announced. He could count on his fingers too. "Show up on time." That was one finger. "Give me your best energy as long as I'm paying you." That was two fingers. "Don't talk behind my back. I hate that." That was three fingers. "And come to me with any problems." Ernie had four fingers in the air. "That's four," he counted—wagging them back at Swimming Pool.

"Deal?" Swimming Pool asked.

"Deal," Ernie agreed, and they shook hands. "Now, will you leave me alone?" he demanded, and shooed her away.

Swimming Pool moved in even tighter. "No, I'm

not leaving you alone. This is my job, Ernie. This is what I do." Swimming Pool nudged Ernie with an elbow and then a shoulder. Any closer and she'd have her arm wrapped around him.

"Ernie," she said softly. "I was very sorry to hear about Mister Doggie."

Ernie said nothing in return—but he did scooch his sunglasses back onto his nose.

"S'okay." Swimming Pool shrugged. "You don't have to say nothing."

And for a moment Ernie didn't. It wasn't like Ernie to cry in front of a girl. But then, after the slightest hesitation, he slowly slumped against Swimming Pool's shoulder.

"Did I ever tell you how he used to cry himself to sleep?" he asked.

"Right. The windup clock," Swimming Pool said. "*Ticktock*. You told me."

"He never did see much of the world," Ernie reminisced. "He was too little. But what a great dog. He had a great smile."

"I know, I know," Swimming Pool replied. She went ahead and slung an arm around Ernie's shoulders. Just friends being friends. "It's okay, Ernie. You can lean on me," she said. "We're a team, right? Thick or thin."

Dusty plunged through the fence with a loud *bang*, kind of surprised to find Ernie and Swimming Pool in the yard. He was hauling his large suitcase behind him, as usual. Only this time, his large suitcase looked kind of different.

"Boss," he said, short of breath. "Made a box for Mister Doggie."

The suitcase was plastered with homemade travel decals, supposedly from around the world, in honor of Mister Doggie.

"But this is your suitcase, Dusty," Ernie said.

"All in the name of art, Boss," Dusty replied. He flipped the suitcase on its side to show it off, pointing to particular features as he described them. "The matador's for Spain. Got an Eiffel Tower and a pagoda. Got a Buddha on the back." This was some of Dusty's finest work and he was really proud.

"What's the macaroni?" Ernie asked.

"Italy, Boss," said Dusty. "I figured we'd let Mister Doggie see the world."

Ernie and Swimming Pool let out a little laugh because the private joke made the box even more special than before.

"*Major Luggage for Mister Doggage,*" Dusty declared, dubbing the work with a title. "I tried to make it kinda funny 'cause I remember how he liked a good laugh."

"I think he'll like it a lot, Dusty. A whole lot," said Ernie. He reached into his pocket. "What do I owe you?" he asked.

Dusty held his hands up to stop any offer of money. "Boss, I'm offended," he said. "This one's on the house. I liked that Mister Doggie. He had a nice smile."

A warm glow traveled between Ernie, Dusty, and Pool. But before they could get all embarrassed and mushy, they heard the loud clang and scrape of a shovel being dragged down the pavement in the alley. Sure enough, Tony appeared at the gate.

"Hey, Mr. Castellano," Tony said. "I was very sorry to hear about your doggie."

"Thanks a lot, Tony," said Ernie. Expecting Tony to hold out his hand, Ernie reached into his pocket for the usual two quarters.

"Whoa, Mr. Castellano," Tony protested. "Your money's no good. This one's on me."

Ernie smiled gratefully at his friends. "You've all been really great about this," he said. "But we can't have a funeral for Mister Doggie."

All the kids protested: "Why not?" "Of course we can." "We have to!"

Ernie held up his hands to silence their protests. "My dad said no more funerals. And besides that, I'm grounded. I'm not allowed to leave the yard."

The kids started to voice more protests, but they all fell silent when the screen door started to open behind Ernie.

It was Red. Ernie's dad. He stepped through the door and onto the back stoop. "I didn't mean to overhear you and your friends," he said to Ernie. "I was just standing at the kitchen window and I happened to hear." Clearly he had been listening to the whole conversation.

"S'okay, Dad," Ernie said, trying to speak as few words as possible. "Doesn't matter. They were just leaving. I was just telling them I'm grounded."

Red sighed and looked off into the distance. "You and your friends go take care of Mister Doggie," he said. He nodded a little bit after that, kind of quiet and sad. And then he slowly walked back inside and let the screen door shut with a *bang.*

Chapter Thirty

A Dog with a Nice Smile

And so, that afternoon, all the kids gathered in the cemetery for one last funeral—for Mister Doggie. Pool stepped forward to deliver the eulogy.

"Beloved Dearly," she said. "We gather today to remember Mister Doggie. 'Course, most of us don't remember Mister Doggie much 'cause he was just a little dog who lived inside."

The kids around the grave all nodded knowingly. What Swimming Pool said was all too true. Ernie scanned the crowd and noticed that almost every kid in the neighborhood was there. Tony, of course. Betty, Jeremy, Kiwi, Gina, Finny and Fanny, Kip, and Sweaty Lemonade Girl . . . even Dion the bully was there.

"Maybe you heard him yapping, but you didn't see him much," Swimming Pool continued. "Mister

Doggie was too little for this big, bad world."

Swimming Pool looked thoughtfully at Ernie before she continued.

"Something else you might not know about Mister Doggie," she said as though she was giving up a secret. "He slept with a clock. A windup clock that went *ticktock*, *ticktock*, and Mister Doggie would sleep thinking it was his mom's heart. It's a little trick you do with puppies."

Some of the kids nodded because they'd used the same trick on their own dog.

"But Mister Doggie was lucky, see?" Swimming Pool went on. "'Cause Mister Doggie figured it out. To Mister Doggie, time was something to hold close."

Swimming Pool smiled gently at Ernie. She was thinking of Mister Doggie, of course. But she was also thinking about Rick, and her own family, and all these new friends she never thought she'd have.

So she said it. "Like friends. And family. To Mister Doggie, time was precious."

Ernie braved an appreciative glance at Swimming Pool and Dusty.

Swimming Pool took a deep breath and brought it all to a conclusion. "So I know it's sad . . . but I think Mister Doggie is teaching us a lesson—and good lessons don't need tears. A good lesson needs a party. And I think we ought to give Mister Doggie the send-off he deserves."

With that, Swimming Pool revealed Rick's

181

tambourine. She held it high over her head and gave it a good shake. Dusty distributed homemade tambourines—pieced together in his inimitable way from bottle caps, pie tins, and ribbons.

Red was watching from the alley. He spotted Ernie with Dusty and Pool. Ernie's face was not quite sad and not quite happy—but there was a radiant quality to it. From where Red was standing, he could see the children running circles around the suitcase—like a wild Greek wedding. As the circle got bigger and the running got faster, the children were dancing, laughing, and banging their homemade tambourines. Sometimes children glow with life.

Red watched for a moment, feeling a little misty.

After all the kids had left the yard, Ernie lingered behind to watch as Tony patted the dirt on the grave. When the task was done, Tony gave Ernie a quiet salute of farewell and dragged his shovel out of the yard.

Ernie sighed. Mister Doggie was gone, and now it seemed like his whole business was gone too. He knew that he should go over to the grave site and say good-bye to Mister Doggie—but it still hurt too much. And besides, what would he say?

At that moment, Red stepped tentatively into the garden. Ernie shifted on his feet. It was still awkward because they weren't exactly on speaking terms.

And maybe that was just as well, because most

of what passed between them happened without words.

Red walked next to Ernie and draped an arm around his shoulder. In his other hand, Red held up the windup clock. He handed the clock to Ernie, and then he reached into his pocket. What he pulled out was a handful of dog biscuits—and the freezer-magnet photo of Red, Ernie, Ernie's mom, and Mister Doggie.

"C'mon," Red said to his son. "Let's go say good-bye."

It wasn't easy, but Red and Ernie walked to the grave site to say good-bye to Mister Doggie—and another good-bye to Ernie's mom.

Ernie set the clock in the grass and got down on his knees to make a pattern on the grave with the dog biscuits. Red handed him the plastic photo frame and Ernie placed it alongside.

They stood there in silence for several moments. And after a bit, it felt very natural for Ernie to reach out and take his father's hand. When he did, Red squeezed down on it tightly. A quick pulse, like a heartbeat. It almost hurt, but only for a second. And later, as Ernie remembered it, it didn't really hurt that much at all.

Red glanced down at Ernie. "Let's go home, son," he said.